©2018 L. A. Gregory. All rights reserved.

Edited by D. Jason Fleming

Cover art by Jennifer Minnis

Chapter One

The gangly vixen froze as an owl's wings flickered overhead. She wasn't long out of the den, and owls would snap up a fox cub as easily as she could gulp a grasshopper. She was quick and clever enough to pluck chickens from their coop, but maybe not enough to dodge talons from above. She glanced around for a bolthole or burrow, ears quivering for any hint of swooping wings.

He's not going to hurt you, said a voice in her mind. It was affectionate with a hint of teasing, like a littermate about to pounce. *He's got a full belly and a warm nest; he's not going to worry about one little fox.*

She wasn't *that* little. But she wanted a full belly too...*I am hunting*, she returned with dignity. *I am quick and clever.*

Hunting what?

Fluffy birds! It felt as natural to answer the voice as it was to test the breeze or play with her littermates. Her mouth watered as she thought of their dusty scent and quick, hopping run--surely almost as much fun to chase as to eat—and she set off again.

They are fluffy, the voice allowed. *But all slow and close together like that, how clever do you have to be to catch one?*

Tasty, she retorted.

There was no reply, but something drew her attention to the invitingly damp scent on the breeze. She'd been further downhill before, where the stream slowed and spread, with frogs and minnows and crunchy little crawlers everywhere.

There might even be ducks. The voice paused, concerned. *Do you* know *how to hunt ducks?*

She planted her feet and all but yapped in indignation. She could hunt anything she wanted. She could take mice and grasshoppers and—well, she'd seen her dam kill a rabbit, that was almost the same thing—and voles if she dug fast enough...but ducks were good. Ducks were *delicious.*

She altered her course, heading for the shallows down beyond the farm with its tempting—too easy!— chickens. Quick and clever indeed; *she* was going to find a nice fat duck.

Kestrel came back to herself in a disoriented wobble, with barely enough time to register the feel of bark under her fingertips before she nearly pitched off her branch. She swore at herself for flying up here in the first place. Safe, yes, but now she'd lost her hold on the bird-shape, and it would take her a few minutes to stop thinking like a fox. A nighttime forest was no place for confusion about which species you currently were.

Rapport with the fox had felt odd. Usually her interventions were far more physical. But the bright little spark of the vixen's mind had called her attention, and Kestrel was supposed to bolster the healthy as well as cleanse the twisted. A healthy fox could kill hundreds of bloodswallows over the course of her lifetime, could raise more kits like herself and start one vigorous line in the tangled mass of the forest around her.

One drop of clean water in the cesspool, more like.

She clambered back down the tree—hands, definitely hands, not feathers and not paws—to where she'd left her pack among the roots. This tangled forest was denser and deeper than the sparse, stony woods of her cliffside home, the air rich with complex scents of leaf must, dozens of rodents, and a distant trace of fox-musk. The night was clear and the sun still setting; if she didn't stop again, she should be able to reach her destination while there was light to travel by.

She didn't. Heavy undergrowth, fading light, and an obnoxiously muddy creekbed slowed her progress until she reached the edge of the farm she'd been looking for well after sunset. It looked well-kept, not like a failing settlement or a bandit haven, and she grinned at the traces of chicken tracks in the dirt. Apparently she and the fox had shared a destination.

She clambered over the barricade around the edge of the barnyard, knocked on the door, and fell back to a safe distance outside the range of a sudden rush from either party. Somebody here had asked for her, but you *never* startled a farmer. Guarding crops and family from beasts, bandits, or poison of one form or another tended to leave them a bit high-strung.

The man who opened the door had a torch in one hand and a long, single-edged blade in the other, but it hung down loosely enough for comfort. Behind him Kestrel could see a young woman with an anxious expression and a pike, and she tried to look harmless.

"Beastblood?" the farmer asked, and she nodded. It was clear enough; the eyes might have been normal, but the hair was obvious. "We asked the Rider to find a greenblood."

Was he reasonable, or hostile? She wasn't obligated to help with something she couldn't directly affect, but walking away could cause trouble for her kind and others. Worse, it would disappoint her family. "I think the Rider just looked for the first one she saw. She told me where to find you—" shouted directions, actually, while struggling to control her sidling horse— "and went on with her messages."

"Hrmph. Don't know that a beastblood can help with this at all." The farmer eyed her skeptically, but he seemed to be thinking rather than reacting. "We think this started with corn. You can't do anything with corn, can you?"

"Well, I can look. Maybe find a way to keep things under control until somebody better-suited can come."

He narrowed his eyes in thought, but nodded. "After sunrise. There's barkhides about and we've been burning back the morrowleaf for years, and I won't risk either of us outdoors overnight. Name's Faryd."

"Kestrel." She dipped her head and followed Faryd inside, where a faint creak and rustle from above indicated a probable wife and children. Whether he'd expected bandits or just someone like her, no one wanted to expose his family to avoidable danger, and there were a few predators clever enough to mimic a knock at the door. Likely his wife was upstairs with a crossbow while the oldest was down here to watch her father's back.

Inside, the farmhouse looked like dozens of others she'd seen, but scrupulously clean and well-cared for, with braided rugs on the floor and carefully jarred preserves gleaming along one wall. The hearth was stone, the floor thick wood, carefully sanded and charred to keep any unpleasant surprises from springing up. The cat on the hearth flicked a single ear at her when she asked it about the family, and stalked off with a disgruntled mental mutter of *my laps my mice not your business.*

"You can sleep by the hearth." The farmer's wariness was abating, leaving the kind of distant courtesy reserved for dangerous professionals. "Warm enough, and the door's sturdy. Anything you need before dawn?"

"I've got something to sleep under, I'll be fine." If the farmer were a little more used to beastblood, she'd have abandoned human form and slept in mental and physical comfort as a cat or a fox. She didn't lose her intelligence when she shifted, but sometimes it was restful to deal only with an animal's simpler needs and contentments.

"There's a hearthrug, at least. It'll help."

She nodded in thanks and unrolled her blanket atop the sheepskin rug, curling up under the felt-lined oilcloth and resting her head on her pack. The room's comfortable clutter and the flickering embers were worlds away from the narrow, airy chamber where she slept at home. But the faint whiff of lye and clean-scrubbed wood at every breath was reassuringly domestic, and the warmth from the banked hearth was enough to set her drowsing in near-feline comfort.

Kestrel woke as the sky began to lighten, rolling up her blanket and stuffing it into her pack before her eyes had cleared. 'Bloods made most people nervous, and it would be most comfortable for everyone if she left as soon as she could. She let the calmly waiting cat outside, its businesslike buzz of *milk milk goats milk* trailing through her mind as it trotted across the barnyard where Faryd was harnessing a ponderous draft horse. The cat skittered around Faryd's ankles, and he raised a distracted hand in greeting as he tried to calm his suddenly shying horse.

"Er. That's me, actually. Horses don't like me."

"They don't?" He put himself between her and the horse, with a reassuring hand on the beast's neck.

"They think I want to eat them. There's a few that are trained to work with people like me, but that takes time that's usually spent better somewhere else." She shrugged. Livestock that was both trainable and uncorrupted was rare and expensive, horses second only to dogs. "So if you tell me where to go, I can meet you there, or we can walk if you'd rather."

"Walking's fine. Thought maybe we could pull some roots with Feather here, but no use scaring the poor boy for no reason." He turned back toward the barn with a penetrating yell that would have done Kestrel's mother proud, handing the restive horse's reins to the pair of tousled children who emerged and hefting the pitchfork and hatchet that had been resting against the mounting block beside him. "All right, bea-- Kestrel. It's not far, and I'd at least like some wiser eyes on this before you go."

She nodded and fell into step beside him, her loose-limbed wolf-pace to his powerful stride, as they paralleled the stream.

"So why is my horse scared of you?" he asked after a moment. "*Do* you-"

"No. At least, I never have. But what we do marks us one way or another. Or several." She flicked a finger to indicate her flyaway hair, mottled shades of brown somewhere between a wolf's brindling and a hawk's barred plumage. "Me, I spend all my time with meat-eaters , and nothing that grazes puts up with me for long, no matter what I look like at the time."

"Hm." Faryd prodded a suspiciously long and exposed root that crossed their path, watching it with pike at the ready until they were both well out of snaring range. A greenblood would have known if it were slumbervine or something worse; Kestrel would rather just dodge it. "So your name's not just something your kin give you."

"Sometimes your kin choose your name, sometimes you change it when you find a better one. My mother apparently couldn't walk outside without getting harassed by hawks trying to feed me, so mine was pretty obvious."

He nodded thoughtfully, and Kestrel felt her shoulders relax a little. Beastblood weren't exactly hated, but they were suspect. In a land where the earth could melt away beneath your feet, where half the plants and almost every creature was a dangerous unknown, people who could speak to or even become animals were intimidating at best. Someone who actually *wanted* to know more was a welcome rarity.

"Good to know. My daughter wants to run away from home and learn to be a greenblood. My wife's ma thinks you all steal babies and change them to be like you. Me, I'd rather talk to one of you and get a different view."

"She wants to what? Nobody's ever decided to be a 'blood that I know of. I don't know how you'd even--"

She heard the rustling well before they left the trees for the cornfield, and the hair rose along her arms. A slithery, razor-edged sound, mindless and menacing; her fingers crooked into claws, thoughts of *cat wolf falcon **out*** racing through her mind.

"Damn," Faryd grunted. "Stuff's spread."

Eyes narrowed to peer through the bushes, she saw a tangle of thrashing leaves, thick-grained and mottled with yellow patches. There were knobby stems just visible through the leaves, in a patch several body-lengths across. Faryd had ringed the corn with rocks to slow it, but roots were already probing through the cracks.

Kestrel blinked. "I've never seen anything like that." Carnivorous plants were common enough, but usually they fed through poison or strangulation. They never moved fast enough to *see*. Where was it getting the energy? "There's no way I can cleanse that, but I can probably slow it down a little. Do you have anything that'll burn hot?"

"I can put the children to gathering kindling. What do you need from me?"

"I can uproot this stuff without getting hurt. I think. If you burn what I pull up, we should be able to buy you a few weeks and *I'll* find you a greenblood to cleanse it." She thought for a moment. "Also, put down your pitchfork for a minute."

She shook the flighty, wary cat-thoughts and hawk-thoughts away and reached for confidence instead. Rippling fur, thick hide, broad paws and resilience; nothing for her to fear here. A moment's concentration, and she dropped to the ground as a dark-furred bear.

Faryd wasn't pointing anything *at* her, but he had a wary hand on his crossbow and a wary eye on the nearest tree. "Can you understand me?"

Kestrel nodded ponderously and shouldered her way into the fringes of the corn field, ears flicking back to catch Faryd's exasperated "*Warn* me, would you?" Something that would normally have embarrassed her only amused her bear-self, and she hooked a paw around the base of a cornstalk and pulled. Loose earth crumbled satisfyingly around her claws, showering down around her feet as roots ripped free. The leaves lashed at her, but slid off her dense fur, and she set her teeth in the knobby stem and worried it out of the ground.

It took a good portion of the morning, but by the time Faryd's family had a respectable pile of kindling gathered, she and the farmer had built up an efficient rhythm. The tainted plants popped and twisted in the flames as Kestrel brought uprooted plants to Faryd, who tossed them on the fire with a twist of his pitchfork. It was going well, but somewhere beneath the bear-born confidence she was uneasy; there was something here she could almost feel, and she shouldn't have been able to sense it at all. Hunger and dull malice, seething at the edge of her awareness – and it wasn't right. Predators hunted, but they didn't hate.

Troubled, she ripped out the last stubborn roots and dragged the struggling plants to Faryd. Whatever was happening was outside her limited experience, but the morning's work had bought time for Faryd and his family. She dug a few furrows through the loose soil, snuffling for any hint of corruption.

Nothing.

She shook herself to settle her fur and released the bear-shape with a twinge of regret. Faryd gave her a bemused blink but held out a hand to help her rise. "This is temporary, you said?"

"Probably. They're slowed, but I can't promise this stuff won't grow again. And I've got to find someone to *actually* help. This isn't right." She thought. "Less right than normal."

He nodded. "I can keep the earth burned down for a moonturn or so. Long enough to get a greenblood out here?"

"I'll need to find one and tell them what I know. Then they can come and stones-please-it get to the bottom of this."

Faryd gave her an unnervingly thoughtful look but didn't question her further; just as well, since she wasn't sure what was nagging at her. But when she prepared to leave that afternoon, after taking care of the usual formalities and answering an appalling number of questions from an appalling number of children, the farmer drew her aside. "I don't know what you saw. Or smelled, or, well, whatever. But this is my land and I know it just as well as you know your creatures, and that's *nothing* I've ever seen before. If there's something worse than usual going on, you tell me, all right? I've spent a lot of years here, but if we have to run, I want to do it before I lose more than just farmland."

She hesitated. Everything other 'bloods told her said she should keep her secrets to herself, but she recognized Faryd's fierce protection of his territory. Any wild creature would do the same, and she couldn't deny this human determination. "Those plants – I felt them and they're hungry. I shouldn't be able to sense *plants*, but they were in my mind, just a little. If you see them again, don't let anything near them, and I'll get help to you as soon as I can."

Chapter Two

Coasting in over a wooded cliffside, Kestrel tipped her wings to spiral down the thermal above her home. From above, it loked like a handful or ramshackle buildings huddled halfway up a sheer cliff, but there were rooms dug several stories deep into the stone, enough for winter lodging for any number of 'blood. Stonebloods mostly stuck to towns and trade ports, and greenbloods were clannish, with sprawling families in sprawling houses; beastbloods were all but nomadic, and most of their houses were built to accommodate ever-shifting numbers and families. Though 'bloods of any sort left people uneasy, beastblood children were harder to raise than most and were generally adopted by a more experienced elder if they weren't born to beastblood parents. After growing up in a mob of adopted aunts, grandparents, and same-age children, Kestrel had long since picked up her mother's habit of referring to any beastblood in the house as a cousin.

Every year, some of the younger cousins began agitating to name the compound something pretentious–"Hawk's Haven" had been the contender last year–but Kestrel never thought of it as anything but home. Built of yellow-gold stone, the compound centered around a broad courtyard, ringed with boulders and deadwood and flagged with dark stones to warm the air and create thermals for flyers. Children and long-term residents lived in a single rambling house, with beds for anyone who was only stopping for a night or two. A cluster of outbuildings, from sheds to a small, solid smokehouse, met most of her family's needs and provided shelter to any travelers brave enough to ask for it; most people were too jumpy around beastblood to risk themselves or their beasts.

"Kess! Dodge!"

And she'd *agree* with them, if more beastblood were like her brother.

She swerved sharply and skimmed over the boy's head as he grabbed for her tailfeathers, swiveling her head sideways to snap playfully at his fingers.

Mostly playfully.

At the eastern end of the courtyard was an upturned stump, roots spreading wide over a sturdy chair and a bundle of canes at its base. She angled to the side and flared her wings to land on it; Crane wouldn't begrudge her a landing on his favorite perch. The sun-warmed wood felt good under her talons, and better a moment later when she slid to the top of the log in human form. "Try that again and I will *fall* on you, shrimp." A mountain cat or one of the smaller bears from a couple of lengths up might make a sufficient impression. Might.

Otter pulled himself up to sit on the log beside her. "'Shrimp' is boring. Find some better insults."

Kestrel bumped a shoulder against him, none too gently. "Please. You've got to learn to pounce better before you'll be worth insulting."

She heard the stifled laugh under his derisive snort and grinned to herself. The beastblood sat more lightly on her brother than on most, showing itself only in large dark eyes and a trace of webbing between his fingers. When he chose to use it, his shapeshifting was as fast and fluid as Kestrel's but more limited; his affinity with creatures of the water was strong, but fish were rarely a threat in a land ringed by impassible cliffs and watered mostly by streams. "I've got a couple of messages to pass on before I can rest. Is Crane anywhere around?" Well into middle age, Crane had never mastered any shape but birds', but his speed and endurance made him an indispensable courier. Half-lamed from a tumble through razor-edged morrowleaf, he needed a cane for everyday use, but he'd taught Kestrel more about flight than rapport with a hundred hawks could have done.

"He got back from Rushwater this morning, but he was still resting last I heard. But I've been helping Mother with caravan negotiations, and this is the first time I've had my head above ground all day."

"Blight. No other cousins around to help?" Kestrel could take any number of hawk-shapes, but for speed and distance there were many others who were better.

"Not lately. I could--"

"I'll talk to Mother and see if she's got any ideas before I have to take off again." She slid off the log's rough surface, landing on the flagstones with a thump. "We're going to need a greenblood, and an experienced one at that."

She couldn't touch another 'blood's mind the way she could an animal's, but she could feel their presence just as they could feel hers, from the cousins' background rumble to Otter's waterfall rush and her mother's calm, steady flow. Home was sparsely populated today, just a few bright points of presence nearby and a few faraway fliers on patrol.

She trotted through the courtyard and into the shaded porch that led to the house proper, opening the rain-warped door with a practiced yank. The long, narrow room just inside was lined with shelves and led to a second, narrower door at the far end. Traveling supplies and outdoor gear loaded the shelves, but nothing they couldn't afford to lose. Even a house full of beastblood couldn't always stave off maddened creatures, and an extra layer of defense never hurt. But today the narrow entryway was lined with straw-filled crates, and she paused for an appreciative sniff. Dried herbs, pungent braids of garlic and onions, and the subtle sweetness of winter squash. She grinned to herself, looking forward to the winter's rest—roasted squash with honey, carving and teasing and stories around the hearth.

Beyond the second door and its heavy bars was the kitchen, vented now to stave off summer heat. A quick sniff of the air inside brought her the smell of bread, traces of yesterday's soup, firewood, and an incongruous whiff of fox-musk, but not the array of subtle scents that would have meant a crowded house. No sharp liniment-smell from Crane, no hint of squabbling cousins; home, at least, was calm. Breezes from unshuttered windows in bedrooms and storerooms tugged at her hair as she passed the doors; they'd be stoppered and barred when the winter storms set in, but when the weather was warm they stayed open to the wind.

Musty herb-smells led her downstairs to the infirmary, a wide but windowless room lined with storage cupboards, with beds at each end and a rarely-used table at the center. Currently, the table was piled with crates, jars, and bundled sheaves, and Kestrel's mother was supervising a trio of long-suffering cousins loaded down with bales and sacks. Tucked against her ribs was a thin fox kit with too-intelligent eyes. Kestrel smiled at the cub with a moment's sympathy. Family wasn't a sure thing for any beastblood, and this child had found a safer landing than many.

"Moth--"

"Don't *drop* that!" Her mother made a frantic grab for a teetering basket of something leafy and sweet-smelling, still keeping the fox kit secure with one arm. "Or I'll never get any more slumbervine from Valerian and then you will *all* have to deal with me."

That got her submissively lowered eyes and hunched shoulders from all three of the younger beastbloods, and Kestrel stifled a snicker. Deer-form or not, even the most rambunctious tended to back down before Roe in a temper.

"I'll just, um, wait?" she asked, eyeing the growing array of dried plants, green plants, roots, and an unnerving basket of still-twitching vines.

"Not likely. You can *help*." Roe handed her a sheaf of something that looked like hay flakes and smelled like the worse sort of swamp. "Here, hold that while I break it up and get it into the jars...got to put you down now," she added to the fox, and set it gently on the floor.

"Yes'm," she said, as cooperative as any of the younger cousins. Kestrel didn't remember – or blame – the woman who'd given her up after months of harassment from raptors trying to flock to her. Roe was her mother in every way she cared to name, and the birth of Otter a few years later hadn't lessened her patience. A compact, dark-haired woman in her forties, she traveled only in emergencies, keeping a refuge open for beastblood. But Kestrel had seen her face down everything from boisterous cousins to winter-starved wolves, and if she *did* choose to shift...well, grazers were fiercer and faster than most people believed, and she'd seen Roe prove that a few times as well.

So she set to work meekly on the herbs, sifting them into baskets and jars while Roe carefully strained tinctures into dark glass jars. Each jar bore a detailed relief of the contents, with meticulously painted pictures of any other ingredients. After weeks of steeping, even a beastblood's nose couldn't identify every component of a formula.

"We need to send a message to Valerian," Kestrel said as they worked. She'd never met her in person, but Valerian had a reputation as one of the wisest greenbloods. If she'd heard of anything like Faryd's problem, she could find a greenblood to cleanse it.

"Well, we *can,* of course. But I think I've talked her out of all the herbs I can this year."

"No, there's--" It sounded absurd, talking to someone who hadn't been there to feel that dull malice. "I ran into some carnivorous plants that were out of the ordinary. I need help from somebody who knows what they're doing, because pulling them up wasn't enough."

"Plants? How did you get caught up in that?"

Kestrel shrugged. "Somebody sent a Rider for help, the Rider decided that any 'blood would do, and there I was." She outlined the bones of the story to Roe, who scowled in thought but shook her head.

"Nothing I've ever heard of, and I don't recall anything like it from my parents or theirs. But we don't generally bother with plants, so it's hard to know for sure. Corn, you said?"

"It started that way, at least."

"Hm. Greenbloods have been culling crops for so many generations that it's hard to imagine a twisted strain coming back now. I can send Crane on with a message, after he's had a day or so to rest, but this may be more complicated than just passing on news. Best that you have a word with Valerian; she might be able to set you on the right trail."

"All right. Let me talk to the caravan master–if I shadow them back to Valerian's steading, that's a little extra protection for them and maybe more trade goods for us next season." With most groups of 'bloods scrambling between one crisis and another, trade was rarely a formal contract, but you could never have too much goodwill. "And maybe she'll know what's going on."

"Maybe. I just don't want you taking on trouble that's not yours to deal with. Our own duties feel like a losing battle sometimes, as fast as the animals change." Alarmed by the change in her tone, the fox pressed up against Roe's ankle, and she hoisted it back up to her hip. "Not a real battle," she said to the kit.

"When did the new arrival show up?" Kestrel held out fingertips for the cub to sniff.

"Tracker rode in with her in a basket about ten days ago. And then bolted the next morning before I could ask him about fostering, because children panic him," Roe added with a wry grin. "Apparently he found her wandering a riverport in fox-shape, and no one knew or would admit to a missing beastblood child. So Tracker left what word he could and brought her here, where she could at least be warm and fed. And come out of your fur when you're ready to meet us," she added to the fox.

The cub tucked her nose against Roe's side, eyes dropping away from Kestrel's.

Delicate questions there, and none she wanted to ask in the hearing of a lonely child. Kestrel had been too young to remember when Roe adopted her, but this little one was at least old enough to walk and talk. "Meanwhile," she said to the cub in a stage whisper, "don't let Mother fool you. Hold out for long enough, and she'll start trying to tempt your appetite with eggs and cheese instead of boring you to deal with oatmeal."

"*Thank* you, Kestrel, for your help with family discipline."

"Happy to help," she said cheerfully, and made her escape while Roe was hastily explaining to the cub about "what we need to eat so we can grow".

Dinnertime was rowdy, courtesy of Otter, a handful of cousins, some of Valerian's drovers, Otter, the fox cub cadging scraps of fish, and Otter. Kestrel regretted her human form and its immobile ears more than once, but she still smiled when she heard the thump-and-hitch of Crane's steps behind her. She hooked a chair out for him with an ankle.

"Good to see you back, flit," he said, lowering himself carefully down and leaning his cane against the table. A keen-eyed man in his sixties, he had a broad, powerful frame and legs half-withered from a long-ago fall into a morrowleaf patch. He still did a beastblood's cleansing work, but only with another shifter guarding him; experience kept him out of trouble, but it couldn't guard him against sudden catastrophe. "How far did you go?"

"I started going north and then looked for trouble spots until a Rider came and distracted me." She helped herself to a generous serving of roasted root vegetables and then added a little more, ostentatiously oblivious to her brother's glare from down the table. "The winterdoves are starting to migrate down, and I kept as much of an eye on them as I could." She couldn't sense them like she could predators, but she'd crossed paths with a migrating flock and shot upward to watch them, mesmerized by thousands of silver-tipped wings. "I can't tell for sure, but they look healthy this year. Other than that...lots of little adjustments, but nothing that seemed to need a bird-shifter."

"Something will come up," he predicted with the certainty of experience. "Just as well. Your m other wants me to take on one of those cousins who are passing through." He gestured to one of the younger beastblood, a curly-headed man slightly younger than Kestrel. She lowered her eyes against an irrational little stab of jealousy; just because Crane had taught her first didn't give her a claim on his training, and the beastblood needed every skilled shifter they could get. "Young Finch speaks mostly with songbirds and we're hoping I can help him expand his skills a bit. So apart from emergencies, I'll be playing baby-tender for a bit. It'll give me extra time for carving."

Kestrel smiled and fingered the bone buttons on her shirt, carved into detailed feather shapes. They'd lasted through four shirts since Crane had carved them for her, and she treasured them despite his efforts to replace them with something newer and fancier. Most of his work went for trade goods, but these were *hers*.

After dinner, Kestrel took herself down to the little cliff-face room that had been hers since childhood. Carved out of the rock below the house proper, a pair of tree-shaded windows kept it cool and airy, and some long-ago beastblood had set perches low on each windowsill. A narrow bed and low chest were all she needed; she wasn't at home often enough to want anything more.

She spent a contented hour restocking her traveling pouch with fresh tools and medicines from the chest. She didn't want to upset the caravan horses by riding or walking nearby, but storing her pack in a cart would let her take to the skies and scout out hazards ahead. It wasn't something she was used to – beastblood were usually too busy with their charges to serve as any kind of dedicated fighter, but muscle, teeth and claws were an effective deterrent against bandits and some of the smarter animals.

She refilled her supplies of numbing salve and the rare, clear liquid whose fumes could bring unconsciousness. She could keep an animal quiescent with her mind along, but magic came only from a 'blood herself, and any healing she could manage with physical tools left her a little more power for the hurts medicine couldn't touch.

She was squeezing an extra jar of salve into the pack when her mother tapped on the door. "Kestrel?"

She looked up inquiringly. Roe stepped inside and sat down on the foot of the bed.

"I need to send Otter with you when you leave. Can you see him back safe from Valerian's steading?"

She blinked. "*Otter*? He can't offer them any more help than the next trailhand."

"I know that. This is for him, not them."

Kestrel settled back to listen, though she couldn't keep the dubious frown off her face.

"There are only a few problems that call for Otter's skills, so he doesn't patrol like you do. He's got to test himself to grow, and there's nothing for him to do it with here."

"Oh, so you're going to test him on *me*."

Roe shot her a quelling look. "He has to to leave safety for a bit and stretch himself. If he takes this step well enough, I can send him to a riverport to work with the traders there." A bleak expression flickered across her face and was gone. "Just because there's little he can prove himself against doesn't mean nothing will come. And unprepared beastblood die."

Kestrel sighed, an annoyed huff that they both knew wouldn't change anything. "He'll pull my hair. You think he's outgrown it, but he hasn't."

"Pull it right back," Roe said in the tone Kestrel remembered from countless interrupted scuffles. "You have to look out for him, not coddle him."

"I don't like it."

"I don't like it either, but he needs it."

Kestrel's wordless grumble would have done credit to a bear sow, but she ducked her head in agreement anyway, and began hoping for drizzle and high winds.

Chapter Three

She didn't get them.

The journey to Valerian's steading was easier than Kestrel had expected, the three-cart caravan trundling along stony trails where the tangled woodland gave way to bluffs and dropped away into spreading plains. The drivers were all armed with machetes, the heavy blades ideally suited to deal with ambush predators and fast-growing greenery; crossbows hung in easy reach in case of any other dangers. The greenbloods Kestrel's family traded with were prospering enough to provide protective barding for the oxen—probably provided by beastblood, who generally traded in fur, bone and meat. There had been a loose alliance between Roe's family and Valerian's as far back as either group remembered, and whatever pelts and ornaments the beastblood produced over the winter would go with the greenbloods' spring caravans to be traded at one of the riverside ports.

Pacing the caravan in hawk-shape just above the treetops, Kestrel could see traces of old stoneblood work: reshaped rock to keep the trails from crumbling away, fused and crystallized stone to guard against erosion. Ragged, narrow strips of stone poked up through the scrubby understory trees, as they did sometimes on the plains or along riverbanks. Some of them looked almost like walls, but there was no trace of quarrying or mortar to make her think of human work, and she'd never heard a stoneblood say anything about them.

Below, Otter paralleled the lead cart on a saddle horse trained to tolerate Kestrel; she couldn't hear him at this height, but from the way his hands flew as he talked with the driver, the trip agreed with him. Between his nose and hearing, both more sensitive than a human's even if he wore human shape, and her hawk's vision, they were able to evade or warn off most dangers. On the second day, she discovered an empty bandit's blind tucked in some boulders just above the trail, and spent a gleefully destructive morning bashing it apart in bear-form. There was little trade at this time of year, but any human predators would find themselves a surprise in the spring.

For the rest, she scouted ahead by day, warning wolves and barkhides away from their path, and rested with the rest of the caravan at night, when the oxen were too tired to do more than stomp a hoof at her in warning. Between her senses and Otter's, the caravan was able to slacken sentry duty, and a relaxed mood spread through the group. By the fourth day she'd stopped getting surreptitious, wary glances from the caravan guards and was getting comfortable enough with the traders to cautiously tease them around the campfire. On the last night of the journey, the caravan leader doled out a share of trade-coin to each of the drivers. Each 'blood made their own coins to signify a favor owed—strong, thin disks of stone, polished wood, or carved bone—but constant barter kept them changing hands. She was surprised and pleased when she and Otter got a pair apiece; she kept a few coins from the family coffers to trade in case of emergencies, but these were the first she'd earned by her own efforts.

On the fifth day, they came down the bluffs and crossed a few miles of flatland to reach Valerian's steading. Even the grass grew steadily thicker and greener as they neared a concentration of greenblood, and new spring-green leaves flickered through the darker summer foliage of the trees around them.

Kestrel nearly took to the skies again the moment the first cart crossed the gates. Long and low, the steading sprawled its way through herb gardens and fields of exuberant crops. Greenbloods crowded on every side, leaving her with chaotic impressions of fluttering, viny hair, knobby joints, and roughened skin tinged with brown or grey – if she'd been in a form that could manage it, she would have folded her ears flat against her head. Beside her, Otter looked just as stunned but more interested. Given the choice, she would've been happy to leave the crowds to him.

"Pull your claws in, there aren't *that* many of them," Otter said in an undertone as they separated from the caravan, following the smell of food in an unspoken plan to find someone who could direct them.

She snorted. "*I saw you jump when those children ran past us.*" Now that the first shock had faded, it wasn't quite the roiling mass she'd believed, but there were still more people in the kitchen gardens alone than Kestrel generally saw in a month, all busy with a sense of purposeful routine that was alien to her. Little children played with wooden dolls and living plants in equal measure, confined to chaotic corners of the gardens where sturdy flowers bloomed, withered and grew again indiscriminately. Greenblood Otter's age were carefully harvesting vegetables; a closer look showed her blossoms already beginning to grow behind any hand that came away with a ripe vegetable. She'd worked with greenblood in the wilds, where they shared her task of cleansing dangerous creatures or those that were too twisted to live, but she'd never seen how they lived at home. Beastblood tended to have wintertime lulls and summers full of frantic activity, and this orderly work left her feeling off-balance.

They passed through neatly organized gardens, trading looks of mutual incomprehension with a knot of young greenbloods trailing an elder and singing what seemed to be some sort of teaching rhyme. Kestrel had had to learn everything she knew through trial, error, and occasional lessons from beastblood more experienced with her particular charges; Otter would have to go through the same process. Plants were slower but no less dangerous in the long run then the animals her people dealt with, but plants weren't likely to bolt or bite you in a panic, so maybe greenbloods had a little more time to try and get it right.

They made their way through the kitchen gardens, past wide, airy stables with draft carts arranged outside them, and finally up a wide staircase with timeworn, shallow dips in the center of each tread. Greenblood defenses were apparently concentrated in the fields and gardens; she saw none of the stored weapons or arrow-slits she was used to in her own home. But the hall atop the stairs was wide and well-lit, opening on either side to sunny rooms stacked with drying shelves and festooned with dangling braids of bulbs or bundles of herbs.

She followed her nose to a kitchen three times the size of the one she knew, where something that smelled tantalizing was simmering on an oversized hearth. A young man with a cane looked up, blinked at their unfamiliar features, and gave them directions to a bunkroom to share after Otter explained their presence. "Dinner starts at sundown, and you can probably find Gran in the stillroom after that."

She thanked him, shouldered her pouch, and puzzled her way with Otter through twisting halls until they came to the unoccupied bunkroom they'd been promised, a narrow little chamber with a pair of bunk beds and a braided rug on the floor. It was barely larger than her room at home, but there was space for both of them to sleep comfortably for a night or two. Crowded as it was, she didn't want to stay long. The cool scent of the stone walls was refreshing after the chaos of human, food, and animal smells outside, and Kestrel quashed a sudden burst of longing for the forests she knew best, where every scent and sound *meant* something.

Otter slung his pack carelessly over the lower bed. "This is different. I like it."

"You would. Although the trip wasn't terrible."

He nodded. "I felt sandspawn near the trails, though. I put them to sleep long enough to get by safely, but we'll have to deal with them on the way back."

"Easy enough. Probably." The tiny, winged amphibians were deadly in a swarm, but they could go dormant for decades at a time, and then even beastblood might not be able to find them. Kestrel could probably dig them out, but it would take Otter to control them.

After sharing dinner at a long table with dozens of greenbloods, Kestrel left Otter talking with a knot of other adolescents and set about finding the stillroom. A sharp herbal scent led her past storerooms and down a twisty little staircase to a cool, windowless room lined with shelves. Inside, an aged greenblood woman was staring narrow-eyed at a slim seedling in an irregular clay pot, all its leaves turned toward her as if she were its source of light. She had a pollen-laden brush in one knobby hand and was carefully skimming it across a spray of flowers, her other hand flexing the same way Crane's did when he was trying to work out a new carving. Her neatly coiled hair still showed traces of black at the tips, but her skin was so seamed and wrinkled that Kestrel couldn't tell if it showed greenblood markings or simple age.

Kestrel took a few deliberately clomping steps over the threshold, unwilling to startle anyone standing near that much expensive glass. "Lady Valerian?"

"Just Valerian. And keep yourself to yourself for a moment." The woman's dark eyes narrowed further still, and Kestrel felt a subtle flicker of power run from her and into the pile of greenery close at the old woman's hand. "...there. Apologies, that's a delicate transfer. My great-grandson was sulking about missing supper and coaxed one of the trees to bear him three different sorts of fruit at once, but he can't figure out how to make the change permanent. So I've been reduced to cross-breeding." Her nose wrinkled in a sneer of professional disgust.

Kestrel blinked. "No wonder Mother'd rather trade with you than anyone else."

"Oh, you're Roe's daughter? I take back...oh, at least half the things I thought when they told me a pair of beastblood had landed on the doorstep."

"Well, I'd rather be on my own doorstep," she admitted. "But I've got a problem I can't understand, and I was hoping you might know something that might help."

Valerian raised an eyebrow, pulled out a stool, and sat down to wait, so Kestrel told her the story of her unfruitful stay at Faryd's homestead. "It wasn't the plants—I've seen vines like that before, just not that strong, but I shouldn't have been able to *feel* them. Should I?"

Valerian shook her head. "Plants don't feel much besides content or unease, and you shouldn't have been able to sense it anyway. I've never heard of anyone with two 'blood talents, and that's the kind of story that would get handed down for sure. So the trouble's likely with the plant and not you."

"But what do you think it *is*?"

"Blighted if I know, child." The old woman scowled in thought. "If you were talking about an animal, I'd almost say it had summer sickness. There's more to plants than flitterers like you think, but they're not tthat complex. More likely to reflect our emotions than to--" She cut off abruptly. "Huh."

"Ma'am?"

"All right. I'll send a few of the grandchildren to look into your farmer's problem. *You* need to start looking for anything else like this, and keep your ears pricked for word of greenbloods acting strangely."

"You know something?"

The scowl deepened, but now there was fear behind it instead of curiosity. "Not hardly. I *wonder* something. Listen: you beastblood reflect your charges, but for greenbloods it's more the other way around. A happy greenblood makes for healthy crops, an angry one makes for plants with thick bark and thorns everywhere. What state would a greenblood have to be in to create something like what you saw?"

Kestrel opened her mouth to answer, but couldn't find anything to say.

"Little fledgling. If we're lucky, this is just an unusual patch of blight. If we're not, and this is caused by a greenblood out of control...well, people aren't at ease around 'bloods at the best of times, and it'll be worse if their crops are threatened. If one of my people is hurt and in danger out there – *find* them before someone else does, and bring them home so I can heal them."

Chapter Four

They left the steading two days later, with a carefully packed roll of oils and tinctures lashed to Otter's saddle and firm instructions for Roe to try them *all*. Otter was excited to be traveling again, his horse was reluctant to leave the abundant grazing, and Kestrel was...uneasy. She stretched her senses as far as she could, in search of anything out of the ordinary, but she had no idea what she was looking for.

Still, the sun was warm, the thermals were strong, and the horse was well-trained enough that she could perch on Otter's saddle horn or trot behind him as a wolf when she tired of flight. Tall grasses waved around Otter's knees as they pushed through the miles, and she only teased him a little bit about holding her pace down to a horse's.

"What about an osprey?" she suggested when they stopped to rest for the night. "They live near water, at least."

"I've tried," he answered shortly, leaning back against the saddle. His expression was carefully controlled. "Didn't work."

"Maybe I could teach you."

He shook his head. "I watched ospreys day in and day out for months. Kingfishers, too. Even swans and ducks. Whatever it is you need to shapeshift, I can't – *reach* them well enough to find it. So I'm stuck with feet or fins, for all the good that does me."

Shapeshifting came easily to both of them, but Otter had far less scope for it. It had always seemed simple to Kestrel—see the world through another creature's eyes, change the mind, and change the body. But it was all intuition for her, and she'd never thought to try it with a creature she didn't already know down to the bones. "Don't sell yourself short. I've seen animals that came up against ripperfish or sandspawn, and it's a bad way to go." People, too, but she'd rather not trouble her little brother with that. "I wonder. You can feel me, and *I* can connect with ospreys. Maybe if we worked together?"

"Maybe. But it's not—I feel *right* in the water, and maybe I should be grateful that fish have less problems than you or Mother have to deal with, but I feel like there should be something bigger. That *I* should be bigger. Not size, just--" He trailed off with a frustrated shrug.

Did he need to apprentice in a riverport? Somewhere that would offer him more challenge, though for herself Kestrel couldn't imagine wanting more trouble than she already had. "We can still try it if you want, if things are slow when we get home." She could alter her usual weeks-long patrol schedule for a while, fly shorter and more intense routes and spend off days with Otter.

"Maybe," he said again. "But thanks for thinking about it."

She tousled his hair, from equal parts affection and the urge to annoy him, and dropped into wolf-shape before he could retaliate. Nose tucked into tail, ears swiveling to catch any hint of danger on the night wind, she slept.

The next day brought them back to the bluffs. Otter's gelding picked his way laboriously up the trail while Kestrel skimmed up the cliff face to perch at the top and wait. She flicked her wings smugly at him when she reached the top, he glared back, and they were off again. Otter led them along their own backtrail until they reached the muddy patch, a half-day's ride from home, where he'd first noticed sandspawn traces.

He slid off the horse's back and tossed the reins to Kestrel. "Hold those, will you? He won't bolt or stomp you, he's trained. Mostly," he added with a grin of pure brotherly wickedness.

"You just *think* you're funny."

Ignoring her, he stared at the patches of muddy ground around them. Technically, there was a stream nearby—a thin, anemic thing that ran only when the rains were strong—but apparently that was good enough for sandspawn. "That's a breeding nest. Trouble next spring for sure. Watch my back."

Kestrel nodded, ground-tying the horse and moving to stand as close as she dared to the muddy patch. Otter dropped to a seat in the middle of it, and she growled to herself. *Showoff.*

But her brother took a slow breath and held down a hand, and a moment later a single sandspawn climbed up on it, a vivid splash of blue against brown skin and brown earth. Brilliantly colored and shaped like a streamlined frog with dragonfly wings, a lone sandspawn could look rather appealing. If you'd never seen what a swarm of them could do to a living being. But the delicate bodies hid gripping claws and razor-sharp little teeth, and most animals learned to avoid the faintest whiff of sandspawn scent.

Otter stared hard at the little creature, and Kestrel could dimly sense him reaching down and out to the rest of the nest. Thoughts of heat and dryness, empty bellies, scorching summer sun, *sleep sleep sleep...* then he shook his head sharply, and the sandspawn toppled off his finger and began to dig sluggishly back into the earth.

"All right, they're dormant now and not just ignoring us. It'll be a few years at least before anything's strong enough to revive them. Is there anything in the area that you can call to come get dinner?"

"Foxes, probably. I'll look as soon as you're done." Any digging hunter would be happy to snap up a nest of dormant sandspawn, but it was far too dangerous for both of them to be distracted at once.

"Good. But-" He peered searchingly at the ground below them. "There's eggs already down there, and nothing to eat *them*. Can I try something? It might take a while."

"It's what we're here to do. Go ahead."

"All right. If I don't move after a while, yell or kick me or something."

"I like this plan."

He flicked an annoyed glance at her, then closed his eyes and plunged both hands into the mud. Kestrel watched as he bit his lip with a frown of concentration spreading over his face.

As the sun climbed the sky, she took the horse's bridle off so it could graze, keeping a watchful eye on Otter. Eyes half-closed, he was scowling ferociously; whatever he was doing, it was hard work. She paced the perimeter of the sandspawn patch to keep herself limber, whether she needed to guard against attack or shake her brother out of a too-intense communion with the nest. But a little after noon he came back to himself with an all-over shudder and picked himself gingerly out of the mud.

"Eggs," he said in a thoroughly disgusted tone, swaying when he tried to step forward.

She blinked. "Eggs?"

"That was *hard*, Kess. Give me a little time." Otter wobbled over to where the gelding stood and leaned against it for a moment, groping for the canteen that dangled from the saddle. "*Every* single blighted egg," he muttered, thumping his head against the seat.

"Good work. What did you do, burn them out?"

"Rebuilt them." He took a gulp from the canteen. "They'll hatch normally and scatter instead of swarming."

"...oh. Stones below, don't stop with just water then!" She dove into her own pack and retrieved a bottle of the restorative she used on animals she'd put through intense healing. "Two swallows."

"That stuff is foul."

"It has honey in it."

"And salt. And every single herb Mother can get her hands on."

"It works, and Mother will throttle me if I drag you home flopped over the saddle, which is more likely than not at the moment. Two swallows."

He glared for form's sake, but drank. Either the argument or the tonic revived him enough to remount the gelding, and Kestrel walked alongside him as they left the clearing. She didn't *think* he'd fall out of the saddle, but she also hadn't thought he'd try to cleanse an entire clutch of unborn sandspawn. Healing was one thing, but Otter had reshaped the eggs all the way down to the tiny, unseen coils that told them how to grow. The eggs might be simpler to cleanse than a young bird or mammal, but he'd made up for that with sheer numbers.

She kept a close, protective distance as Otter threaded his way along the narrow trail that led up the cliff to home. So she was close at hand when the gelding snorted and laid his ears back at the smell of smoke from up the trail.

From home.

Chapter Five

"Catch up," Kestrel ordered, and dove off the trail in a flurry of feathers. She shot up the cliff face and on to level ground, weaving through the trees around the courtyard until she could get a clear view. She kited up to a branch to look, huddling close to the trunk to stay unobtrusive. The courtyard was silent and undisturbed, the house echoingly empty to ears and mind alike. At the far end, the open door swung back and forth.

Stones below us. Her skin prickled as the feathers on her head lifted. She would almost rather have seen signs of a fight than this silent emptiness.

She dropped from her branch, hitting the ground on four tawny paws. Her feline nose caught the smell of smoke, a thin, acrid reek of burned food and dying embers from indoors. She twined through the scrubby trees to the top of the trail, waiting for her brother. When she saw the gelding scrambling up the path, she stepped out into clear view to avoid spooking the horse.

"The stable's burnt out. No dead horses," Otter reported in a low voice, sliding out of the saddle to crouch beside her. "Is there anything out there?"

She signaled a "no" with a sideways dip of her head. Roe had taught them early how to communicate simple information in shapeshift form; it was crude and clumsy, but enough for an emergency.

Otter glanced at the bristling fur on her shoulders and tail. "Is it safe to go in?"

No. Scout.

"Want me with you?"

Yes.

"Shifted?"

No.

"All right, lead the way."

She crept around the edges of the courtyard with Otter several steps behind. Smoke from inside stung her eyes and nose, but she caught no trace of strangers. One beastblood scent, though, strangely blurred—her head snapped up from the ground, muzzle wrinkling back to test the air in a single deep inhalation.

Not here, not *now*. But she couldn't deny that familiar scent. Head lowered, hackles lifted, she paced hesitantly to the side of the courtyard where Crane lay face-down.

"Stones--" Otter choked behind her, but not in disbelief. Beastblood saw death early; the sick feeling in Kestrel's belly was grief and loss, not denial. She crouched over him with her muzzle to his hair, and it was a long moment before she could bring herself to leave the cat-form behind and turn him gently over. There was no sign of violence, apart from his outflung arms, and only a trace of decay, too faint for a human nose to detect. He was dressed in the comfortable clothes he preferred at home, with no gear for either travel or battle.

"I think he fell," Otter said softly. "There's a cane back by his chair, and the way his, um, his arms are out..." He trailed off, jaw clenched against threatening tears.

Kestrel bit back her own. No time for grief or fear, with her family missing from a danger she couldn't identify. "If he was taking off and his heart failed him...maybe. No sign he was fighting.

"There's no sign *anyone* was fighting. How did it get like this?"

She squeezed her eyes shut. "What first, how later. We'll come back and tend to him as soon as we can."

Otter nodded reluctant agreement, and Kestrel returned to cat-shape, the smells of smoke and decay growing stronger as she shifted. She could catch faint scents of her mother and the other beastblood, but no horsey smell or leather-metal tang of armor to indicate bandit presence. No blood either, she realized after a moment.

Watch behind, she signaled to Otter.

The weapons in the entry room were untouched. Inside, the untended kitchen fire was burning down to bitter-smelling ashes, scorched stew crusting the interior of a heavy pot above it. She almost shifted back to douse the fire before remembering that this was no longer friendly territory.

But not exactly hostile, either. Their home was empty from courtyard to stables as far as Kestrel could tell. Otter searched the shell of the stables while Kestrel prowled in search of scent trails; she found the marks of fleeing horses, but no prints of human or animal feet. Otter had no more luck, and Kestrel found him picking slowly through bits of untouched tack when she returned.

"I don't know what happened up top," he said. "But all the horses are gone. One saddle and bridle missing for each one, like they just decided to go on an afternoon ride."

She shifted out of the cat-shape, feeling strangely vulnerable without fur and claws. "I've got no idea what happened either. I don't smell blood, I don't smell any strangers, and I don't hear anything at all. It can't have been bandits, not with all the weapons still in place. Twisted bears or wolves *might* be strong and smart enough to break in, but not without drawing blood or leaving some trail."

"So what do we *do*?"

She had to stay calm. *Had* to; she was the oldest and they were in danger. "We—we load up your horse with whatever he can carry and head for safety. Valerian can give us space to rest while we figure out what to do next."

"But we don't know where Mother is. Or anybody."

She took a shaky breath. "No, we don't. And whatever happened to them, I don't want it happening to us."

"I don't want to leave!"

"Neither do I!" she snapped back. "But I can't see anything, or smell anything, or—*anything* to tell me what happened. For all we know, the stone swallowed them. We save what we can, we find a safe place, and *then* we start looking."

He growled, but followed her up the narrow stairs from the stables. The bedrooms were empty, a few recently used but most smelling dusty with long disuse, and Kestrel passed them by after a cursory sweep. She looked away from Crane's collection of carvings and straightened his unmade bed without really thinking about it; it took both her and Otter, neither meeting the other's eyes, to check their mother's room for anything useful. There was a small bag of traders' coins from all three 'bloods laid carelessly on the stand by her bed, and Kestrel eyed it uneasily. More evidence against bandits and for...what?

With Roe's store of coins and all the lightweight rations from the kitchen carefully packed away, they were clearing the stillroom of usable medicines when Kestrel heard a rustle. She flung up a hand to warn Otter and froze, straining ears and mind.

No sound now, but a faint ripple of emotion, *sadscaredlonelysad*. And a hint of animal warmth, all but drowned out in the sharp medicinal smells that surrounded them. Picking her way through the bottles scattered on the floor, Kestrel took a cautious step after the wisp of scent.

"If you're beastblood, I want to help," she said in as calm a tone as she could manage. Glancing around them, Otter set his medicines down and turned to watch her back. "Do you know what happened?"

That got her a sudden little flinch of a sound, and she and Otter both pinpointed it: the heavy chest where Roe stored empty flasks and bottles. Looking dubious, Otter gestured her forward. She narrowed her eyes at him and laid a wary hand on the lid. She didn't *think* it could be a trap, but the day had shown too many impossibilities for her to take chances. Tensed to spring backward, she lifted the lid. And found a little girl hunched against the confining space, with ragged black hair and fox-gold eyes in a dusty face.

"Oh, *stones*," she said in relief and dismay, lifting the child out. "You're Mother's little cub, aren't you? The one I saw before I left with Otter?"

A nod.

"Can you tell us what happened?"

She froze.

"...all right, we'll try later on. We've got to leave here for a little bit," she said to the girl. "Otter, you walk her down to the stable, and I'll finish up here-"

The child went utterly still, eyes dilating to a thin rim of gold around enormous pupils. Kestrel blinked. "All right, Otter, *you'll* finish up here. I know a campsite we can reach by sunset if we try."

Awkwardly, she left the house with the little girl a half-step behind her, surveying the unaccustomed emptiness with wide, dismayed eyes. Keeping herself between the child and Crane's half-visible body, Kestrel tried to comfort the little girl, but a few halting and unsuccessful attempts convinced her that silence was better for both of them. The child did reach for her hand halfway across the courtyard, and released it to tentatively stroke Otter's gelding when they reached the path down.

Otter arrived shortly after, a clinking satchel of bottles slung over his shoulder. "That's all of it. Let's go if we're going."

In strained silence, they loaded the horse with as much as it could carry. Beastblood could travel lighter than most, and Kestrel was grateful; it left more room for the trade supplies that were their only asset. Medicines, a double handful of coins, a few choice furs, and a jar of honey that Otter produced and handed to the beastblood child.

"She likes honey. I thought it might help."

Kestrel nodded and let Otter lead the gelding down the narrow path while she brought up the rear. Was there a scent trail she'd missed somewhere? A hint she'd overlooked? Every step away was an effort, but she didn't dare risk the three of them against whatever had overcome a house full of beastblood.

They made their silent way down the switchbacks that led to level ground and hugged the low cliffs that ran north, finding nothing more dangerous than a patch of slumbervine. Kestrel took to wolf-form, ranging in wide circles around the other two until they crossed the path she remembered. It was hard to find from the ground, a thread of a gravelly trail leading back into the hills, but she gestured to Otter to follow and trotted unerringly uphill. Halfway up was a crevice in the rock, sheltered from wind and predators and softened by generations of passing beastblood. When Kestrel had first come here, she'd found a stash of bedrolls and a tarpaulin sized to fit the narrow crack above them; since then she'd added a water bucket and a cache of spices. Sometimes she wondered what the next 'blood to find this place would leave.

She stretched on tiptoe to retrieve the tarpaulin and unrolled it in Otter's general direction. "Fire goes outside, you and the cub sleep inside, and I'll stay out to keep watch."

"*First* watch. Do you think it'll be safe to light a fire?"

"I think-" She thought that she craved the warm, homey light like water after a long run, and that the little fosterling had likely never spent a night in the wilds before. "I think it'll be all right. We couldn't find sight or scent of trouble at home, and that's miles behind us now. And I can take all of night watch. I've got sharper ears than you."

"Kess. I don't want to go, but if we have to, we should do it right. We'll need you alert tomorrow."

She looked down. He was right, she knew that perfectly well, but she didn't want to sleep. Maybe it would be different after food and a few hours on watch.

With a discreet fire kindled, Kestrel nibbled at the jerky they'd brought from home. Otter devoured his, and the little beastblood worried hers down with what sounded distinctly like a growl. She should talk to the child, she thought distantly, but they were all exhausted in ways beyond the physical.

So she scuffed out the fire after a wordless meal, helped the others set up their bedrolls, and left the crevice to keep watch in wolf-shape. Her throat kept tightening around a howl that she refused to voice; it wouldn't reach her missing kin, and it would make Otter and the little girl feel worse. Back to the embers, she stared out into the trees and tried not to think.

Chapter Six

Otter woke her midway through the night and stared at her pointedly until she took his bedroll and slept. When she woke just after sunrise, she found that the little 'blood had turned back to a fox overnight and was curled in a ball between her neck and shoulder. "Not one word," she said to Otter, and sat up with difficulty. The fox cub shook herself to blinking, annoyed wakefulness as the morning chill penetrated her fur.

She gave the cub another piece of jerky and bread with a dollop of honey before kneeling to pack up the bedroll. "We need to get moving."

"Kess, I was thinking." There was a touch of unease in her brother's posture, like a bear cub not long out of the den. "It's safe at Valerian's, but she can't help us find Mother or the cousins."

"No, that has to be up to us." And blight take her if she knew how to do it.

He hesitated. "If we change our plans, it doesn't have to just be us. I don't think."

Kestrel opened her mouth, closed it after a moment, trying not to defend her half-formed plans just because they were *hers*. "Then what are you thinking?"

"Get to the river, head upstream until we reach Threeshores, and use the coins to hire a Rider. They're *trained* to find 'bloods when they're needed, so they might be able to find ours."

"That's...all right, that's better than circling back and looking ourselves." She stretched to put the bedrolls back on the ledge where she'd found them. "We'll have to find somebody to look after the little one while we're hunting, though."

"No." It was tiny but definite, and Kestrel turned to see the little girl staring at her with a stubbornly set chin.

"It's too dangerous to come any further than you have to. We'll find somebody nice to take care of you." Somewhere.

"No. She was nice." She flinched when Kestrel stepped toward her, but didn't move.

"Child, we can't—oh, *stones*." Kestrel sighed explosively. "Let's just go. We need to reach Threeshores before the food runs out, and I can't guarantee good enough hunting to keep us all fed. Can you ride with Otter?"

A nod.

"Then we'll cut west toward the river and figure it out from there." She could travel through the most dangerous territory without missing a step, but children left her baffled. Maybe she'd go back to fox-shape and Kestrel could just carry her by the scruff.

In silence, they threaded down the narrow trail, Kestrel taking to the trees as a marten when the leaves became too thick to see through. Traces of hunter-thought were all around her—foxes drowsing away the morning, a distant wolf-pack, a falcon far above—but none of them held any memory of what had happened to her home. A far-off bear, fat with summer feeding, radiated discomfort from joints that had never grown quite right, and she bit back the impulse to turn aside and tend to it. Too many other priorities, too many dangers she couldn't see, and her kin right in the middle of it...

The silence didn't last long; by the time the sun rose above the hills behind them, Otter was talking to the little girl where she perched atop the gelding's saddle. The steady flow of words was clearly meant to soothe and entertain her; she wasn't talking back, but seemed to be listening with interest.

--sometimes it's birds, or grazers like Mother, or something really complicated. Crane says his grandfather worked with small creatures and it didn't matter what else they were, mice and songbirds and snakes, and there's stories of 'bloods who could just talk with reptiles or just deer or...whatever. 'Bloods too weak to do other magic usually learn to be Riders instead, but we know you can shapeshift, so you'll probably just need to study as many creatures as you can and see which ones...sort of pull at you. Or come looking for you, like Kestrel."

She made an annoyed trill at him and dropped down to land on the path in human form. "I can turn into a fox like you," she said to the child. "When you're older, I can show you how to talk to them."

"Oh. Did your parents run away from you too?"

Kestrel took a moment to choose her words. "No, but my mother was scared because hawks and falcons kept following her around, so she gave me to Roe to raise. Then Otter showed up a while later, which was fine until he learned to *talk*." She traded a familial sneer with her brother. "He's still learning what he can do, but when he's grown he'll keep twisted animals from hurting people and heal them if he can. People trade us back medicines and supplies that we can't hunt for ourselves, and we get along well enough even if they're scared of us sometimes."

After that, she listened to her brother ramble with rather less than half an ear, searching the trees for anything that might endanger the three of them. Ever since Faryd's farm, the rustle of leaves put her on edge, and the memory of Valerian's fear had her studying every branch she crossed and every shrub below her for signs of something more malicious than the usual magical scarring. There was no way to know how long that taint might have been manifesting in the wilds before it had crossed to cultivated land where someone could notice it.

Her ears pricked at a sudden giggle from the little beastblood, who seemed as surprised as anyone else at the sound. She'd paid only vague attention to the story Otter was telling—something about a distantly related boar-shifter—but the little girl looked more animated than Kestrel had yet seen her.

"...and he refused to tell anybody what happened, but Grandfather says he never dared to ask for truffles again after that."

She listened as Otter began another story, more aware now of what her brother was doing. With Roe and the others missing, there was no one to show the girl what she could do or warn her about the dangers she might face. Greenblood and stoneblood children could learn rules from an experienced teacher, but animals were far less predictable, and beastblood needed to apprentice to someone with similar skills. Right now, the two of them and their stories were all the little fosterling had.

"So we don't always fit in with regular humans," Otter was saying. "But they don't get to fly or swim like we do, and most people never go far from home because it's just too dangerous. A smart beastblood can go *anywhere*." He grinned up at Kestrel as she trotted to the end of her branch and leaped.

That much was true. Sudden disappearances like this one would have meant death for most people, even for other 'bloods. Even if they'd survived by sheer luck at first, they'd managed to save a little bit, and might still be able to locate their family. They had a destination and the beginnings of a plan.

For today, it was enough.

Chapter Seven

"Little cousin, we've got to call you *something*," Otter said the next day, as he led the gelding at a careful walk through the trees. As t hey left the cliffs behind, the soil grew richer and deeper, the trees taller and easier to ride through as they shaded the underbrush away. They were tracking a stream that led down to the southern branch of the Rush, making their way down to the river itself. From there, Threeshores should be an easy day's walk. "'Hey, you!' isn't very helpful in an emergency. Did your friends or parents call you anything you could go by?"

The child scowled and shook her head.

"Fox could be all right," Kestrel suggested. "Just don't let it limit you."

Otter picked his way over a tangle of twisted oak roots, and Kestrel eyed them suspiciously. Old, twisted patterns marred the bark, but it was grey and seamed with age; if there were any taint in the tree, it hadn't been active for years. She felt as baffled as a wolf pup snapping at butterflies; no trail to follow to the family she wanted back, and no safe den for the ones with her. The urge to take to the sky and just look aimlessly made her fingers fan out into wing-shapes at odd moments, but she didn't dare leave the other two unprotected.

"Don't like Fox," the girl said after consideration. "People threw things at me, before the big bird man came and gave me food."

"Who, Tracker?"

She shrugged. "He chased the people away, and then I came to your house." A pause. "I liked being a fox there."

"But not anywhere else?"

Her face fell. "Not by myself."

"Well, you're not by yourself now," Otter said. "But we really do need something to call you until you can choose your own name. Tracker found you at one of the towns on the Rush, didn't she? What about River for now. Or Fisher?"

She thought. "I could be Fisher. For a little while."

"Good enough." Otter gave her a brotherly grin without any of the reservations that Kestrel would have been unable to hide. "That'll make it *lots* easier to tell stories about this trip when we catch up with Mother and the rest."

That won him a tentative smile, and she seemed to settle more comfortably into the saddle.

Kestrel felt something tugging at her throughout the day, but the sun was slanting into late afternoon when the rough bark seemed to fade away under her paws, all her senses overwhelmed by a distant, powerful surge of wolf-thought. A whole pack's worth of images and sensations—not pain precisely, but something wrong, somethiing twisted—*stones cutting pads, dig for safety, feed the cubs so they'll grow to dig, knobby ribs and wasted muscle, dig dig dig-*

Lost in the pack's mind, she froze. Otter went a few steps forward before he noticed her sudden stillness. "Kess?"

She didn't bother coming down before shifting shape, but with pack-thought flooding her mind, it took her a moment to remember words. "Trouble. I can't pass this by. I can't—I can't even *think* until it's done with, they're too loud." The pack was hammering at her thoughts now, their obsession too consuming to let them feel her presence. "Can you, um--"

He laid a hand on the branch where she sat. "We'll keep going along the stream until you can catch up with us. Unless you think you'll need help?"

She shook her head. The wolves' disorder was mental more than physical, and she would have no trouble finding them.

"All right. We'll set up camp at sundown. Fisher can handle a short watch after supper, and I'll take the rest until you get back."

She managed a harried smile and slid off her branch, shifting on the way down. She bolted into the underbrush as a wolf, tapping into the pack's memories to find the path she needed. A deer trail *here* with branches whipping across her face, a cut down into a narrow ravine *there*, a scramble up a rockfall to run along the narrow ledge beyond, then *down* and she slid into a clearing full of pebbles and scrubby grass.

The earth of the wolves' clearing crumbled beneath her paws. What should have been a normal den was a formless mass of tunnels turning and twisting underground. Nowhere to rest, no safe place for pups, and no intelligible plan. The wolves weren't digging with a purpose, but the need that drove them ran as deep and strong as the drive to hunt, to mate, to howl. A breeding pair, a lone adult, three younger siblings and a pair of pups, all of them echoing with the same compulsion.

She sat down, tipped her head back, and howled, putting enough power behind the call to draw them to her even through their obsession. They straggled up from holes all over the clearing, starving-thin and disoriented, the pups trailing after their mother and yipping halfheartedly for her attention. The older wolves held back, eyeing her uncertainly. The pup's father stayed below until she called him out with another tug of power; subtlety wasn't really possible with a single instinct driving the entire pack. She could feel famine from all of them, feel the sting of cracked and bleeding paw-pads, and worse, feel the urge to run back to the endless digging.

She slid her gaze politely away from the oldest male's and yawned deliberately; courteous signals enhanced by her own abilities to put the pack at ease. Or at least as much as they *could* be. The compulsion that drove them was a natural instinct run out of control;

the pups weren't quite overtaken yet, but they were befuddled and distracted by the lack of normal care.

Start with the parents; while she held them in her mind, their healing would make it easier to reach the others. If she failed them, the pack would remain one more threat to the forest's precarious balance, would bear more litters of pups to grow up trapped in their own minds.

With the pack's focus on her, she eased back into human form—one more layer of protection against falling completely into wolf-thought—and focused on the oldest female. If Kestrel healed her but failed elsewhere, her next litter might still have a chance.

Help me hunt, she told the she-wolf with images rather than words: tantalizing scents, intriguing rustles, a reliable pack-mate to flush the prey. The wolf was ravenous but had been ignoring it for a long time; Kestrel tamped the hunger down completely so she would have one less distraction to deal with.

The wolf tossed her head, breaking eye contact. *Den. Dig!* Kestrel reached out with hands and mind, drawing her attention back. It might be only mental, but it was a hunt all the same, discovering what was twisting a mind as complex as a wolf's. Sifting through the mass of memories and sensations was a delicate job, but slowly she caught a glimpse of the path she needed.

The wolf had been misborn, with no overt defects but a subtle *something* going wrong deep in her brain. All her instincts were stronger than normal, strong enough to override intellect and adaptability. If the hunting drive had been triggered before the denning one, she might well have led her pack rampaging through the forest until they died of starvation among untouched kills. Her mate had come to her young and conformed to her behavior, and she'd passed the compulsion on to their pups.

Finding the problem was slow but easy. Undoing it would be...slow but hard, most likely. Kestrel soothed the wolf with images of rest—sunny afternoons, marrow-rich bones, icy mornings with her tail warming her nose—and set to work. Wounds were easy to heal, physical twisting less so, and mental scarring was tricky at best. This was somewhere between the two, a subtle change deep in the she-wolf's brain where the normal flow of tiny sparks changed to something thick and tangled and *wrong*. She dove for it like a hawk on a mouse.

The wolf blinked drowsily as Kestrel slowed the feverish pulse of her instincts, suppressing the drumming *dig dig dig* with an ordered progression of desires. Hunt, eat, play, sleep; she carefully laid the new pattern down, reinforcing it in the center of the wolf's brain to give it the comfort and force of habit. The tumbling flow of images that made up the wolf's thought slowed, eddied, and began to ease into the new configuration she'd built. One last push, a burst of power to heal the bleeding paws and give the she-wolf the energy to hunt, and Kestrel released the contact.

The wolf sagged. So did she. One cleansed, the rest of the pack still to go. But she'd done the hardest part; the rest would just be repetition. Exhausting repetition, but at least she knew how to go about it now.

The pack father was easier, with only habit to break; the younger wolves were more pliable, and one of the pups fell asleep against her leg while she was working. When she withdrew from his mind, he blinked at her before taking a mouthful of her trousers and worrying it experimentally.

The moon was high overhead when she finished and the pack was exhausted, the lead pair most of all. She set them all to sleeping with a gentle thrum of power, doing what she could to strengthen their bodies for a normal life. Their obsession had let everything from mice to deer breed out of control, but at least the hunting would be easy when they woke. If there was nothing else going wrong with this patch of wildland, the pack would be able to keep their territory stable and healthy, and the next beastblood through this area would have less to do.

She sat back on her heels, scrubbing her palms over her face. Magic only looked effortless if you weren't the one doing it. Her muscles were tight, her feet were going numb, and her focus was exhausted after hours of work. If she tried to fly back to Otter, she'd blunder into the first tree she passed.

With one last check of the sleeping wolves, she stood, stretched, and carried the pups to rest against their mother, indulging in a quick stroke of their velvety fur. Then she slumped down into bear-form, checked the wind for the scent of water, and set off to find Otter's campsite.

Tired as she was, she didn't bother with paths, or thorns, or much of anything beyond a straight line. Even if she risked flight, the trees were too thick for her to find her family from the air. But the bear's nose was keen enough to keep her on track, and when she caught the horse-honey-jerky smell that she'd become familiar with over the past days, she swerved and made straight for camp. Blurry bear-vision caught a faint metallic glint in the starlight, and she stumbled to a halt when she remembered that Otter had a crossbow and wasn't necessarily expecting *her*.

With effort, she shifted back to two legs and marched the last few lengths toward the banked fire. "All better," she informed her bemused brother. She circled the fire, found an unoccupied bedroll, and curled up next to Fisher without another word.

Chapter Eight

They trudged into Threeshores late the next day, Kestrel back on her feet after spending most of the day sleeping as a marten draped over Otter's shoulder. Slouched in the saddle, Fisher perked up as the wooded terrain gave way to footpaths, to rutted roads, and finally to cleared land and a wide cart-route at a shallow ford.

Threeshores sat at the split of the northern and southern branches of the Rush, a massive outcropping raised from the riverbed by long-dead stoneblood. Narrow catwalks and three-cart-wide bridges spanned the river on both sides, leading to smooth stone streets above the piers where fishing boats and traders' barges tied up to unload. To Kestrel's forest-trained eyes, it rose dizzyingly tall, honeycombed with hollows that served as shops, storerooms, and homes. She could see the long-ago stoneblood's hand in the smooth lines and careful design, but it had evolved over the centuries, with newer hand-hewn niches and passageways and the occasional wooden addition attached to create new stairs or bridges. Or stranger things; both the younger beastblood watched with a touch of envy as a porter two stories up tipped his bale of cloth down a steep chute and slid down it himself a moment later.

Kestrel was above such things, of course. She was mature and responsible and not tempted at *all*.

The footbridge swayed across the river and opened up onto a cobblestoned road, sized for a single cart but crammed full of people with a bewildering array of gear, clothing and companions. Hunters from the northern hills with dog-drawn travoises piled with furs, a girl with a pushcart laden with spicy-smelling kebabs, an elderly man hurrying ahead of them with a box of sharp-scented herbs...Kestrel gave up on tracking anything but her own people and dropped back a step to keep a steadying hand on the gelding's saddle. This energetic chaos was less unnerving than the intense, ordered activity of a greenblood steading, but the waves of scent and sound still made it hard to keep her mental footing.

Banners and carved signs rose above them – a knapsack for a general supplies store, an abacus for trade arbiters, and a multitude of loaf-and-bread images for inns. It was hard to pick out the horseshoe sigil of the Riders in the turmoil of colors, but once she found it, she nudged Otter and pointed. "We should head up there once we've got the horse stabled."

He shook his head. "Food and sleep first. Not everybody's three-quarters nocturnal like you."

"Spoilsport."

"And we'll get a better hearing from the Riders if we wait until they're not all tired and surly. And till *I'm* not all tired and surly."

She acknowledged the point with a noncommittal tilt of her head, and they worked their way down the tangled streets until they found cramped but clean stables near the waterline. Otter looked around curiously. "Wonder why they don't stable livestock on the mainland and free up more space for the traders?"

Kestrel shrugged. "Safety. They're likelier to keep trade routes open if everyone knows their horses and oxen won't get eaten. If things get dangerous here, they can just drop the bridges and be safe from everything but, oh, a swarm of swamp lizards or something."

"Beware the invasion of the snapping turtles," Otter intoned solemnly.

They traded a stack of squirrel pelts for a night's stabling, with promises to renegotiate if they stayed longer, and left the stables to find space for themselves. Otter pulled their pack of medicines and trade goods from the saddle, slinging it over his back while a pair of energetic children unharnessed the horse. Footsore as the rest of them, Fisher grumbled when they lifted her down from the gelding's back, until Kestrel scooped her up to ride piggyback.

"So we sleep because *some* of us stayed up all night and walked all day-"

"Almost all day."

"I was awake all day and it counts." Otter eyed her sidelong to see if she had any further comments. "I need sleep, so does Fisher, and you probably do too. So we'll see if anyone will trade furs or medicine for a room and try to s—hey, *food*."

They stopped in their tracks at the smell of hot fish, and turned in unspoken unison to trace it back to its source. They found it in a stall near the water's edge, where a burly man was frying fish while his children trotted full plates out to slat tables lined up along a narrow, torchlit pier. His silver-tipped hair and hulking shoulders showed more than a trace of beastblood; if she tried, Kestrel could sense a hint of his presence in the crowd. He likely didn't have the power to shapeshift, and was unable or unwilling to become a Rider, but she could feel a trace of ursine power eddying around him like a stream.

After a glance at the popping grease, Kestrel talked the man's bored daughter into trading a pot of salve for fish all around. Laden plates in hand, they squeezed past a trio of bargemen, a beleaguered-looking clerk, and a knot of greenbloods hunched over their food before finding what could charitably be called a seat for two along one of the benches. All three of them squeezed in anyway.

The fish was mealy, mild and rich with a peppery bite in the breading; after days of jerky and occasional small game, the hot meal felt like it filled her down to her toes. Fisher snatched a piece without bothering with her tine, crammed it into her mouth, and blew on her scalded fingers before pouncing on another bite. Roe would have scolded her, and Kestrel had a guilty hunch that she should as well, but she felt far too much sympathy. Besides, scolding would keep *her* from eating.

Otter gave her a distinctly unsympathetic look. "Never mind that, Kess. There's no adults around and nobody has to yell at her about snatching food."

"I'm an adult," she objected.

"You're not an adult, you're a sister."

"Who could roll you right into the river."

"Which I can *breathe*."

Outmaneuvered, she stole a piece of his fish just to prove she could. "So what do you even know about hiring a Rider? I don't know what to do with one; they always come looking for me and then their horses run away with them."

"A little bit. Mother and Crane were thinking I might work as sort of a liaison with them if my skills didn't...broaden a little. Which they haven't." He scowled at his plate for a moment. "They have halls in most towns, and they're supposed to get paid by the people who need them to find a particular type of 'blood. So if we can trade the furs and medicines for expenses while we're here, we can save the coins for a Rider. See if they can sense any beastblood in—um, in distress, and that should help us narrow it down."

Neither of them wanted to say what came next. Kestrel said it anyway. "And if we find bodies or—just nothing—we go home and start to rebuild."

"We do." It was a bare wisp of sound. "But we need to know what *happened*. What could have been strong enough to take a half-dozen beastblood without a fight?"

"They didn't fight." Fisher's next bite lay forgotten in her fingers. Her eyes were dilated more than the torchlight would allow. "I would have been braver if they fought. But they just walked away."

"All of them?"

She swallowed. "The nice lady stayed for a little while. I think she was scared to go outside. But then she started talking to nobody there and she put me in the chest."

Kestrel took a slow breath, as careful as she'd ever been when stalking dinner or setting a bone. "What did she say when she put you in?"

The little girl's forehead creased, and Kestrel wrapped an arm around her shoulders as Otter left his seat to stand protectively behind her. "Stay there, don't move, be quiet. And then I couldn't understand her because she was talking too fast, and she kept talking until she closed the lid, and that's all that happened until you came!"

She buried her face in Kestrel's ribs. At the fish stall, Kestrel felt a tug of curiosity and worry from the bearish cook; he urged his reluctant daughter in front of the cauldron and shouldered through the crowd toward them. "The little one all right?"

"For right now," Otter said. "We've got some people missing, and we're all worried." Beastblood died early far more often than any other 'blood; if Roe were truly dead, it would hurt deeply, but the unknown nagged at Kestrel like an itching half-healed wound.

"Animals? Or bandits?" He gestured out to the woods across the river, barely visible now in the deepening twilight.

"We don't know yet. We came here to organize a better search."

"Can't hurt, I guess," the beastblood said slowly. "Just tread lightly around the greenbloods; something's got them in a twist lately." He held out a hand so broad that Kestrel half expected to find fur and claws on it. "I'm Deeproot. If things go badly for the little one, find me and we'll see what we can do for her."

"Finding a safe place to sleep would help for tonight." Kestrel stood up, hoisting Fisher up to her hip when the little girl showed no inclination to move. Otter shouldered their packs as the older beastblood told them where to find lodging. Kestrel lost track on the fourth set of stairs he described, but Otter seemed to be following the directions reasonably well.

They trudged up two staircases, around another one, and across a third that seemed to have started out as a footbridge, winding their way through passages grown or cut in the massive outcropping. The floors were polished by centuries of use, but some walls were stoneblood-smooth and others bore the marks of chisels and hammers. Torches supplemented pools of light that came down through ancient skylights, and Kestrel could hear faint conversations from behind doors of wood or laminated hide. It was utterly alien to the forests and hills she knew best, or even to her little cliffside room, but she was beginning to get used to that.

They found a hostel—she *thought* it was the right one—in a lofty corner of Threeshores, where the distance from the docks kept prices low. It was nothing but a handful of rooms set in stone, with soot-streaked walls from years' worth of lanterns and a cubbyhole for the owner to track guests, but it was enough for a safe night's rest. Two bunks and a chest for their gear all but filled the little room; Kestrel stuffed the chest full to keep the floor clear if she chose to sleep in a shifted form.

She laid the sleeping Fisher down with a pillow and blanket, and sat down on the chest besides the door to kick the boots off her weary feet. Otter was getting ready to sleep, but slowly, with a thoughtful gaze on the little girl. She had an unnerving idea of what he was thinking.

"We're *supposed* to be finding a place to foster her," she said.

"I know. But...it doesn't feel right, Kess. Does it feel right to you?"

Slowly, she shook her head. "And I don't know why. But her blood family didn't want her, Mother's...wherever she is...and she's only started to trust me and you a little." She spoke slowly, trying to puzzle out her own meaning. "If we walk away, she'll probably be safe but—you're right, it doesn't feel like what we should do."

Otter frowned. "She's going to need a teacher just like anybody else. Whoever that is, if she can't trust them..." He trailed off with an expressive shrug.

"If she can't trust them, she may not learn the skills she needs. Or she may just disappear and be a fox for the rest of her life. If she goes, then we've put her in danger and we don't even know what it *is*. What if the thing that took Mother gets us too?"

"And? What if it gets the two of us and we never come back for her? She's one of us. She's a better survivor than some merchant child just from that."

"Hm. She's been perfectly clear about what *she* thinks, but she doesn't know what she's up against."

Otter snorted. "Neither do we. She knows how to shift a little, and we may be able to teach her more. She's beastblood, Kess, and we're the closest thing she has to kin."

Kestrel sighed, torn between dangers. "Yeah. She's beastblood. She comes with us."

Chapter Nine

They spent the next day disposing of the things they'd salvaged from home. Beastblood were uniquely suited for living wild; even Otter, with limited experience, had sharper senses than most and almost as much training as Kestrel. So she sorted out the bare minimum through the packs she'd brought from home, saving three bedrolls, the lightest of the rations, and her medical kit, and showed the results to Otter.

"I don't like it, that's all we've *got*." He scowled. "But there's nowhere we can store it, so we'll have to make the best of it."

"And it's easier to move fast with coins than with a bunch of stuffed packs."

His grimace testified eloquently of his reluctance to agree with her, but he shouldered his half of the trade goods without argument, and they made their way down to the docks to find the arbiter Haila recommended. Kestrel kept a wary eye both on Fisher and the crowds around them—they had little enough to steal and plenty of ways to defend it, but she didn't want to cause an incident by sprouting fur and claws on a busy street.

The shops they passed evolved from shabby to opulent as they got closer to the docks, culminating in a row of stores with richly-colored drapes set around smooth glass windows. Kestrel stole glances as they passed; silky clothes flowing like water in one display, impossibly detailed glass figurines in another, jewelry and musical instruments in a third. Another level down, and the dockside shops took a turn for the pragmatic, leaving them among tools, boating gear, and travel supplies.

Fisher tugged at her hand, pointing to the wooden sign that swung over the heads of the crowd. Carefully carved with an arbiter's scales-and-abacus design, it was polished to a high gleam and edged with copper-flecked paint. Kestrel nudged Otter, and shouldered clear a path for them with Fisher trailing in her wake.

Inside the office, a fine-boned woman in her fifties looked up as the door chimed. "What can I do for y--oh." She blinked. "I was expecting fishermen at this hour, not beastblood. My name's Kelleen. Are you looking for supplies, or coin?"

"Coin." Kestrel started forward with her armful of pelts, but Otter stepped on her foot and maneuvered in front of her.

"We've got tanned pelts, medicines, and a few other odds and ends," he said with a smile he never aimed at family. Though the cookie-cadging one he used on Roe was a close cousin. "We need to trade for traveling gear, and Deeproot at the docks recommended you for help."

"Mm." Kelleen riffled experienced fingers through the stack of beaver pelts that Otter slide to her, looked critically at the vials and pots they'd taken from the storeroom, and nodded at the string of carved bone beads that Kestrel hesitantly handed over. Crane would rather she used his handiwork for help than hang on to it, but she *missed* the old man.

She looked over the shelved while the arbiter muttered to herself about hundredweights and percentages. The tiny office was crammed with crates, pelts, metal ingots, and a bewildering assortment of loose goods, with a discreet back door hinting at a storeroom carved in the rock. Worn shiny with use, the abacus on the desk was clearly no mere symbol, but Kelleen hardly seemed to need it as she counted off weights and numbers to herself. A quick drumming of fingers on her desk, and she focused on the beastblood again. "I can offer you decent coin for the furs and other goods, but for the medicines you'll probably want to deal directly with a healer. There's a group of them that work together up near the tip of the city; they might want to talk to you."

The healers' collective was a wide space on the top level of Threeshores, on the opposite end of the Riders' hall. Sharp smells of herbs and alcohol wound through the walkways long before they reached the compound itself, and all three beastblood were absently rubbing their noses by the time they reached the main door. Fisher wrinkled her nose and looked dubious when the door opened with a subdued wash of scents from cloth, soap and beeswax, but Kestrel hoisted her briskly up on one hip when it looked as if she might balk. "One more stop and then we'll see about dinner, all right?"

The little girl subsided, with a faintly predatory gleam in her eyes that told Kestrel dinner had better be *soon*, and looked silently around. The hall was mostly open space, its walls set with shelves and closets. Folding screens made temporary enclosures around a few empty beds and a handful of desks and tables, but most of them were tucked away against the walls to make room. An upper balcony ringed the wide room, closed doors barely visible beyond the railing.

An herbalist invited them them in with a wave of one hand from behind a stack of folded linens and introduced himself as Dremen. A wiry man in his fifties, he had potion-stained hands, tousled grey hair, and clear green eyes that widened when he got a good look at them.

"Oh, you're *beastblood*!" he cried, taking in Kestrel's amber eyes and brindled hair with a look of surprising delight.

She blinked. "Yes. Why, does something need chasing?"

"Oh, no. Not at all. Here, can I see those?" He gestured at one of the satchels slung over her back. Bemused, she lowered it down and laid the contents across his desk while he called to another herbalist over his shoulder; she strode briskly up, followed by a pack of girls and young women who eyed the newcomers curiously. "What I'd like to do is pick your brains."

"Pick my...?"

Otter snorted. She glowered at him; if *he* spent his time surrounded by predators, he wouldn't necessarily think it was a figurative term either.

"I'd like to see if you've used these before and find out what results you've gotten, whether you've noticed anything unusual, that sort of thing. Normally we get deliveries from the river trade or from the greenbloods, but we learn a lot more from the beastbloods when one of them shows up."

She took a moment to pick her way through the torrent of words. "I've used all of these at one time or another, but why's that important? And why does being beastblood matter?"

Dremen's initial flush of excitement began fading into a relaxed teacher's stance. "Greenbloods tell us what a plant can do, but beastblood can actually *see* the effect on animal bodies, and sometimes what they see helps us treat human troubles better. So if you've got the time...?" He trailed off with a hopeful look.

She glanced out the window at the lowering sun. "A little."

He grinned and dove on her stock of medicines like a hawk on a mouse, and she spent the next hour describing Roe's medicines and their application in more detail than she'd believed herself capable of. Halfway through, the girls who'd been following the older woman around—apprentices, she gathered from their posture and tentative air—scattered at the mention of chores, taking Fisher and a bemused Otter with them. Kestrel watched them go with only a twinge of worry; the ones who weren't cooing over Fisher were cooing *at* Otter, and neither one was really cause for concern.

For her, at least.

She showed Dremen the way she packed her medicines for a prolonged patrol, with salves to heal burns and draw out poison, decoctions to ease birth or soothe aching joints, even the pungent solution of spirits that she used to cleanse infected wounds. The last got an impressed whistle from Dremen as he wiped his watering eyes.

"I thought your people had sharper senses than most. How do you stand that stuff?"

"I only use it for physical work, not magical, and I dilute it with water."

"Hm." He essayed another cautious sniff. "We had a beastblood working with us when I was a boy, and he used a weaker solution that smelled like this. Said that infected wounds felt like his—his patient, I guess?--was under attack by a pack of smaller animals, and the wash seemed to weaken them. That's not something *we* can notice, but we tried it for a year and had a lot fewer infections arise."

Kestrel thought. "That sounds reasonable. We add a few herbs before this is ready to go—" She counted them off rapidly, and both Dremen and the apprentice-mistress scowled in concentration, committing the information to memory. "And it's more effective than spirits alone."

Dremen nodded. "We'll experiment and see how that works. We've been drumming the bit about alcohol wash into apprentices' heads for the last thirty years-"

"-and most of them are deeply upset to learn that we don't mean ale or wine," the apprentice-mistress interrupted with a smirk. Dremen sighed with exaggerated patience.

"So hopefully we've seated that knowledge deeply enough that it won't be forgotten in a generation or two. Train a few dozen apprentices, and if you're lucky a few of them will get it right."

Kestrel couldn't imagine teaching that many; beastblood children could learn the basics from their parents or fosters, but all the complexities of animal bodies and behavior were too much to teach on more than an individual basis. Still, when she compared it to her own years following older beastblood on patrol through woods, rocks, and rain, she couldn't help but envy the airy spaces and organized cupboards of the healers' compound. She followed Dremen as he showed her through the hall, from carefully arranged storage chambers to the large upper rooms set aside for teaching apprentices or treating the ill and injured.

"We generally don't have that many patients at once," he explained as he added her stock of salves to a cupboard engraved with an image of a squat, corked jar. "But when there's a winter cough or a bad brawl—or stones-defend-us a bandit raid—we can do more with our space and supplies pooled than we could working alone, and people know where to come for help."

"Instead of having to comb the forests to *find* your job before you do your job," Kestrel said with a wry grin. "If there weren't so many people around, it'd be nice to work somewhere like this for a change."

"It'd be interesting to have a 'blood healer. I've often wondered why there's never been anyone to work with people the way you do with plants or animals."

"That's--" Relaxed from the healer's curiosity and open manner, Kestrel wasn't quite able to suppress a flinch, but she kept the unease out of her voice. "That'd be too complicated, for one. And I've never seen humans with any sign of corruption. Injuries from something that's *been* corrupted, often, but nothing that's part of them."

"Come to think of it, I never have either. Still, I'd love to see what someone like you could do."

Kestrel was saved from an answer by the reappearance of an aggrieved Otter, pulling Fisher by the hand. One of the apprentices—or possibly all of them; they had the seamless communication of a wolf pack—had taken it upon herself to trim the little girl's ragged hair into a sleek, dark cap that suited her pointy features. Now she was tipping her head curiously back and forth to get used to the feeling.

"I think sandspawn were easier to deal with," Otter muttered in answer to her inquiring look. "Took everything I had to convince them Fisher wasn't their own personal doll. I barely got away before they started trying to clean *me* up."

She glanced at him sidelong with a building smirk. "I'm sure Dremen can spare some of that spirit wash for them..."

"It's so sweet, how you think you're funny. Can we *go* before they find me again? They said there's a whole dormitory full of them."

"I liked them!" Fisher blew her newly-cut bangs off her forehead with a puff of air.

"Not helping," Otter hissed.

Grinning, Kestrel turned to settle accounts with the healers, pocketing the handful of greenblood coins with a tentative feeling of confidence. They'd paid for the Rider's services already, and this would help them with gear and rations. And after that...well, she'd deal with "later" when it came.

Chapter Ten

The Rider's hall was located at the very peak of Threeshores, high enough that even Kestrel felt uneasy when she first looked out the windows. Glass windows, too—necessary at this height to keep out the wind, but she couldn't begin to guess what they must have cost. The interior was spare but comfortable, with clusters of chairs gathered around low tables and simply-patterned tapestries lining the walls. The furnishings were worn but proudly maintained, with carefully polished wood, neatly mended cushions, and patterned tile laid over the bare stone floors.

"So you're looking for beastblood but you don't know where to start?" They'd been greeted by a retired Rider named Haila, a lean woman in linen and leather with greying hair and hazel eyes. From the way she spoke, there was a sharp mind behind those eyes, but neither warmth nor hostility that Kestrel could detect. She couldn't sense the Riders the way she could other beastblood, but this many of them created a subtly shifting pressure in her mind, like the wavering shadows of leaves on a windy day. It was disconcerting, and she hoped it would fade away with only one Rider around.

"We're looking for family. And we know where to start, back down south. They just disappeared, and we haven't been able to find a sight or scent trail. Nothing was stolen, at least nothing we could see, and Fisher was there but she hasn't been able to tell us much. I've never heard of anything like this, so we really don't know *what* clues to look for-"

"Otter." She stepped forward with a touch to her brother's arm. The Rider's frown of concentration was taking on an irritated edge, and Kestrel took a moment to organize her information as a hunter would prefer it. "We're looking for between four and eight beastblood; one of them is my mother. They vanished without a fight while my brother and I were away from home, six days ago or more."

"No more than eight," Otter added. "Fisher wasn't hungry enough when we found her for it to be more."

Kestrel nodded. "My best guess is that they headed for the plains – most of the hills near home are impossible if you can't fly. If there's a Rider we can hire, we'd need to come with them to be sure of who we find."

"Hm." She looked them over with particular attention to Fisher, who was apparently planning an assault on the chairs so she could look out the window. "Come with me. And don't let your little sister climb on anything."

"I wasn't going to *really,*" Fisher sulked.

"We're a long way up, and you can't fly. No windows for you." Kestrel hoisted her up and followed the Rider down a short hallway. They passed a handful of young girls in a simpler version of Haila's garb, and one travel-stained man of about Crane's age who flicked them all a weary nod before disappearing into a side room. Kestrel caught a scent of horse and hard work from all of them.

Haila led them into what looked like an unusually roomy armory, dominated by a bulky, irregular stone table at the center. Three Riders were studying the table, and casually made room for her when she set Fisher down and came to investigate. It was shaped like a rough oval, twice her height from end to end, with a lumpy surface that didn't look quite random. Rough and jagged at the edges, it smoothed out toward the center, marked by a trailing ribbon of glossy, blue-grey stone. The branches thinned into delicate strands near the edges, and she traced one of the lower ones with a curious finger until--

"Otter, look, it's home!" She gestured toward a miniature duplicate of the hills she'd soared over all her life.

He squinted. "What?"

"Look, there's the road to Valerian's, and there's the cliffs and the spring." She pointed them out. Looking more closely, she could see a tile carved with a pawprint where her house would have been, and a similar tiny leaf marking Valerian's steading. "If it were bigger, we could probably even find our sliding rock. It's home."

"It's *everything*." Haila's detachment had yielded to a certain professional pride, a smile tugging at the corners of her mouth. "Mountain to mountain, as far as anybody's explored and made it back to tell. There's one like it in every major Rider hall. The stoneblood who first made it called it a *map*."

Kestrel stared in delight, still picking out places she'd seen from the air or through the trees. "How old is it?"

"Centuries." The stoneblood created them so we could plan patrol circuits and have a good idea where to find a given Rider at any time." She showed Kestrel a carved pattern of interlocking loops, centered on a tiny rock mound.

"Oh, and that's Threeshores."

Haila nodded. "That means we can keep track of which Rider is on which circuit and when we can expect them back again. Smaller outposts have a copy carved in wood, but those deteriorate after a few years, even if we have a greenblood try to preserve them. They're still helpful, though, if only to help our apprentices learn the terrain while they're carving new ones.

"So somebody comes in looking for help because the local sparrows have developed a taste for blood, or the crops are overrun with slumbervine, or whatever other disaster crops up when nobody's looking , and you use the...the *map* to find the Rider closest to them?"

"Usually, yes. Or a Rider with the strongest affinity to the 'blood that's needed right then. They find one of you, send them to fix the problem, and get back on their circuit. Now, do you think you can show me where you think your people went?"

Kestrel leaned forward, tracing a wavering line west from the hills that marked her home. "This is the trail we mostly use – it's wider and easier than the rest, so if they were running or trying to find help it's the most likely choice. It's a little less than two days' walk until the country opens up a little, and if there's no trace of them by the time the plains start then...I don't know where to go look after that."

"That's what we're supposed to help with. We're not successful with every search, but you'll have better luck with one of us along than not. If you're willing to contract for his help, I can call in one of the younger Riders that I think will suit you. He's not as experienced as some, but he's fast."

Kestrel glanced back at her brother, who nodded. "Without someone to point us in the right direction, we're down to just searching aimlessly at this point. How much will it take?"

Between the three of them, they argued their way to a price that didn't leave them entirely destitute. "If we're agreed, I'll call Athren in to meet you. He's been on the southern circuits recently, so if anything untoward is going on that way, he'll have a better idea than we do here."

At Kestrel's nod, Haila crossed to a cabinet on the far wall, and took out what looked like half of a river stone. The smooth oval shape was sheared cleanly away on one side, marked with a smear of red paint along the fractured plane. Dozens of others were neatly lined up on shelves to either side, each painted a different color or pattern. "We provide rooms for ill or injured stoneblood in exchange for activating these tokens to call a Rider on circuit home. Athren's got the other half of this one. If nothing's in his way, he should be back here by midday tomorrow. You'll want to discuss food and gear with him—Riders almost never travel with company and you'll probably all want to pack accordingly."

They spent the afternoon seeing to Otter's gelding. By the time the sun went down, Otter was blinking drowsily whenever they stood still for too long, and by the time they'd eaten—fish again; the familiar beastblood-sense from Deeproot's stall was as close as she'd felt to home in days—he was drooping down to prop his chin on his hand at the first opportunity. With a flush of guilt, Kestrel herded them all back to the hostel. Her brother hadn't had much time to recover from the journey here, and he wasn't as used to travel as she was. She decided she'd made the right choice when he tousled Fisher's hair, toppled onto the farther bed, and rolled himself into an immovable lump of blankets.

Which still left her with one sibling to deal with.

"I'm bored." Fisher bounced experimentally on the end of Kestrel's bed. She'd been placid for a while, long enough for the other lodgers in the hostel to settle and sleep, but apparently watching Kestrel recheck their gear was no longer enough to amuse her.

"How are you bored?" Kestrel demanded in a whisper. "We ate supper, we walked, and we visited the stables. You should be sleeping, not bouncing."

"Borrrrrrred." A trailing thread on the blanket caught the little girl's eye, and she started unraveling it with one hand.

Kestrel blinked. "Well, what do you usually do when you're bored?"

"I'm not hungry. And I'm not tired. And I'm not scared. So I don't know." She wound the thread around all her fingers and examined the resulting flipper-shape with interest.

"Hm." At home, they had a few simple games for winter nights, but she hadn't had the time or interest to pack them. Then again, at home they would have been trying to find a teacher to help Fisher identify and sharpen her talents. Here, that had to be her and Otter. "Hold on a minute. And leave the poor blanket alone."

She trimmed the lamp down, woke Otter long enough to get a groggy acknowledgment from him, and turned back to Fisher. "Come on, I'll teach you to explore like a beastblood."

Fisher's eyes brightened, and she bounced out the door behind Kestrel. "Where are we going?"

"Anywhere we want." She crouched down to the little girl's eye level. "Use your nose, use your brain, and *ask for help* if you think you're in trouble. Think you can keep up?" She took in a breath, concentrating on thoughts of speed, cleverness, adaptability, and let it out again through a fox's masked muzzle.

Fisher stared, giggled, and shifted to match her. Kestrel grinned at the cub, turned, and trotted down the darkened hall, her brush lifted in a follow-me flag.

The torches outside their hostel were largely doused for the night, leaving just enough light for a human to walk carefully. Fox eyes saw more clearly, and the two of them raced through patches of light and darkness, ears flicking to catch every detail. Noises of the settling town rose around them: rodent squeaks, muttering from an occasional clerk or merchant working late, thumps and grunts from dockworkers far below. Kestrel wasn't sure how anyone *ever* managed to sleep here.

They squeezed under a wooden stoop to avoid the notice of a pair of women trudging home—pushcart cooks, Kestrel judged from the smell of dust and spices that clung to them. Beside her, Fisher scuffled in the darkness for a moment and emerged dusty but triumphant, clamping a colorful scrap of ribbon in her jaws. Kestrel snatched a trailing end, and they tugged each other down the hall and halfway down a flight of stairs before Fisher dropped her half and bolted away in pursuit of a moth.

She let the cub explore at her own pace, clambering down stairs and squeezing through railings for a closer look at everything that caught her fancy. She'd often felt the strange pleasure of seeing things as no one else could see them, soaring above cultivated fields or creeping into a panther's den, but it was stranger and stronger here, seeing this beehive of a city turning quiet and still. As the porters finished unloading, she could hear the ripple of water from far below them, catch the echo of quiet conversations instead of the roar of trading and argument that dominated the air during the daytime.

They slunk along a rickety walkway hammered into place behind the dockside food stalls and squeezed out between two stalls to find themselves at river level with a cool drift of weeds-fish-mud teasing their noses. Fisher eyed the boats at anchor and the handful of late diners and crouched down playfully on her elbows. Kestrel's nip for her scruff missed as the cub bounced up from floor to bench to table, yipped at the weary dockworkers chewing their way through a late dinner, and bounded off into the darkness with her tail flagged high. Kestrel flattened her ears and trotted after her.

Side by side, they made their way across a wide stone bridge and jumped to the ground below, Fisher's jaw dropped in a cheerful canine grin. The muddy soil was cool under Kestrel's paws, a faint, fishy scent rising to meet her nose. She tilted her head at a muted sound below her, whuffed for Fisher's attention, and dove with paws flying on the hidden burrow. Fisher scrabbled gleefully along beside her, and they dug up a snapping crawfish in a spatter of silt and water. Kestrel pinned it with a paw before showing the younger 'blood a proper killing blow, and they shared the sweet, cool-tasting meat in comfortable silence. Beyond the circle of torches at the docks, Threeshores was going dark, with nothing but starlight casting a faint gleam on the river and the stone mass towering above it. Kestrel had seen bigger hills, and a few taller trees, but the weight of all those sleeping lives made the shape in front of her loom larger than any of them.

Fisher nudged her and trotted back onto the bridge, shifting out of fox-shape to dangle her legs over the edge. "It's awfully big."

"Threeshores, or the river?"

She thought. "Everything?"

"I know what you mean." Accustomed to a bird's perspective, she'd been thinking of the journey here as a short and simple thing. But the world was so much more complicated from the ground, and she didn't know *what* would face them when they left Threeshores. "But we've had some time to rest, and whatever comes next, we can adapt to it." They had to.

Chapter Eleven

Kestrel slept through most of the next morning, and woke to find Otter and an obnoxiously cheerful Fisher smirking at her. But they'd saved her breakfast, in the form of spiced oat cakes and a pitcher of milk, so she forgave them after a muted growl at no one in particular. "Been busy?"

"A little. Exploring with Fisher, but we stayed on two legs so people wouldn't throw things at us. Did you really let her bark at a tableful of porters?"

"I didn't *let* her. She's fast."

Fisher giggled.

"Also, getting my horse tended to and pricing traveling gear at the stores."

Mouth full, she tilted her head inquisitively.

"It's more complicated than it looks. Good stores are about a level up from the docs, and everything's all fancy, and the prices are fancy too." He snorted. "The first one I tried wouldn't even let me in. The upper levels where we are have all the used and broken stuff, and they'll trade for *anything*, but most of that didn't seem worth it. So we'll probably need to start at the top and work our way down a level or two to find what we need."

"I will never understand what you and Mother see in all this haggling."

"Comes of being a hawk half the time. It's a little different when you can't just swoop down on what you want."

"It's a little more complicated than that-" she began indignantly, but Otter grabbed her arm and started tugging her toward the door.

"Come on, we're supposed to meet that Rider soon. We have to make sure he talks to you first and not Fisher, or he'll probably turn around and run straight back for the stables."

They hiked up a steep little staircase and across a swaying catwalk to return to the Rider's hall, where Kestrel kept a preventative hand near the scruff of Fisher's jacket. The junior Rider manning the door gave them a cursory examination and a wave toward a group of chairs, where they waited until Haila appeared with a young man in tow. Whipcord-lean and close to Kestrel's height, he had an indifferently trimmed mop of dark hair and a skeptical scowl. Grey eyes and unnaturally smooth skin hinted at stoneblood ancestry, but the sun-creases around his eyes and the loose, wary stance were all Rider.

"Athren," he said with a nod of introduction. And you're the three 'bloods Haila wants me to shepherd around?"

Otter bristled; Kestrel didn't. It wasn't quite bluff and wasn't quite anger, and she'd seen the same attitude from any number of uncertain predators. What Athren acted like *after* the posturing was over would be far more important. "Exactly," she said blandly. "Haila said we need to discuss gear with you."

"Likely. What'd you bring with you?"

"Two bedrolls and a set of saddlebags."

He blinked. "And?"

"A horse."

"A *horse.*" His posture was a mute plea for patience. It felt oddly refreshing to see it on someone else. "Yes. You will need gear. Lots of gear. Might as well get started now."

They started. And continued. Up and down the entirety of Threeshores, as far as Kestrel could tell. First to the stables, where Athren gave their gelding a knowledgeable once-over, nodded in cautious approval, and ignored them all in favor of a brief and incomprehensible conversation with the nearest stable hand. Otter excused himself to see to the horse's tack, and Kestrel paced Athren back up three levels in pursuit of some obscure bit of camping equipment. After passing four general goods stores, two tack shops, three leatherworkers and a bakery that didn't meet the Rider's specifications, Kestrel began to suspect he was testing her. So she increased the pace.

"I suppose you'll want a tent?" Athren asked as he finally motioned them to a halt at a leather shop somewhere beneath the Riders' hall.

"Tarpaulin," she shrugged. "We're all used to sleeping rough when we're not at home."

"Even the little girl?"

"Fur helps."

"What about injuries?" He held up a leather knapsack with a dizzying variety of pockets; Kestrel itched to fill it up, but there were more important things to buy. "You'll need medical supplies in case something happens, and unless we get really lucky really fast, we'll be spending a lot of time far from help."

"I *have* one of those." At his disbelieving look, she started ticking off the contents on her fingers. "Bog moss, comfrey oil, needles, catgut, willow extract, a glass blade—I had a trocar, but then there was a thing that happened with a bear--"

"You people are all mad. You leave home with a couple of saddlebags, but then you carry around a medicine kit like *that?*"

"It's not all healing hands and mental tricks. Sometimes it's easier to fix the problem directly, and the only time I use my power is keeping the animal calm. You wouldn't believe the number of bones I've set or births I've helped with."

"Really?" He blinked, suddenly looking much younger. "I thought beastblood were mostly—defensive, I guess. Keep the animals under control when they got vicious."

"That's the part everyone sees. A lot of the time it's just trying to keep the healthy creatures in one piece so they'll have more young and edge the tainted ones out over time. Sometimes you use medicine, sometimes magic, sometimes just planning ahead--" How could she explain what it was like to feel a kit's bending bones strengthen under her hands, or trace a subtle flaw back to its source to ensure painless hunting and healthy cubs? "You have to think, make sure you're not strengthening one set of animals at the expense of the others, or else you get populations out of control and have to do even *more* work in a couple of years."

"Huh." He frowned. "If it helps, there's an apothecary down near the docks. She mostly sells to the dock captains, but they all swear by her. Might have some stuff worth a look."

She spent a contented half-hour in the apothecary's shop (down four sets of stairs and over two bridges), a dim little nook just above the docks, and utterly failed to resist temptation when she found a set of curved steel needles to replace her bone ones. Even Athren seemed interested in the convolutions of a complex little distillation set, tracing the curves with a thoughtful finger while the apothecary's assistant wrapped Kestrel's needles.

"Stoneblood work," he explained, examining the tubing with a critical eye. "Glassblowers can do some amazing work all on their own, but pair it with someone who can control sand and it can get a lot bigger. Or more complex. Or both. I got to do some work once for a family of brewers in town, with a still about like this but about twice as tall as you are. Would've loved to see it in action."

"You had to escort them somewhere too?"

He shook his head. "Apprenticed with the glassworkers for a while, until I started showing enough sensitivity to be a Rider. I liked it; you got to see all the different parts of Threeshores, not just the fronts the traders put on to get you to buy things."

"But you wanted to be a Rider worse?"

"Not really," he said with a deliberate shrug. "But you can't have too many Riders, and there's plenty of glassworkers. I got talked into it. I like the horses, though."

"Someone has to, I guess. Mostly they're too busy trying to run or trying to kick me for me to decide whether I like them or not."

"Yeah. We're going to have to get you down to the stables to see if any of the regular string can deal with you."

From the apothecary's store, they backtracked to a leatherworker (up two staircases, around a spiral ramp, and across a rickety catwalk) for a broad swath of treated hide that could serve as a roof or a ground cloth, and then to the stables reserved for Rider use. The path to the stables (after three flights of stairs, a completely unnecessary alley, and a gated wooden bridge) stretched over the river, a railed walkway with an unnerving amount of water showing between the slats. On the interior side, the walls were studded with farriers, ironmongers, tack shops, and something that smelled like a granary. Kestrel tipped her head for an exploratory sniff; something from in there smelled edible to *her*, never mind the horses.

"We'll need to buy extra rations for the horses," Athren informed her, swerving toward the open door of the feed store. "Your gelding's a tough little beast, but he can't make a long journey on grazing alone, and I know mine can't."

"How many oats will we need?" she asked, picturing a pack horse loaded nose-to-tail with sacks of grain.

"We cooked up a recipe for feed bars a long time ago. Concentrated stuff, but use enough honey to hold it together and the horses don't care. I'll order enough for two trail horses, and then I'll need you in the paddocks for a little bit." He gestured over his shoulder to the barn behind him, a single long line of stalls with a gleam of daylight at the far end.

"Why?"

"Horses are hard to manage around you, you said. I need to see which of the ones I know will still work."

She kept pace with him through the barn, where assorted horses snorted, shied, or snapped at her, and out to the paddocks. Built on wide, sturdy platforms that extended over the river, the sand-floored circles were wide enough for a trot or careful canter and ringed with movable jumps, ramps, and other creations Kestrel couldn't even name. "For training?" she asked.

He nodded. "Got to be able to stay in the saddle through anything. They save the *really* dramatic horses for apprentices, though. Survive five or six months of a hysterical colt trying to bounce you off his back because somebody wiggled a rope, and all of a sudden you really appreciate a nice, jaded trail horse."

"I wouldn't know. I've never met one."

Athren vanished into the stables and came back out with a skeptical horse trailing him, then went back in for two more. Kestrel stayed carefully still while he trotted circles around her on each of them: a big, rawboned beast with a lot of plowhorse in him, an aging mare with scars trailing down her shoulders, and a nervous-looking, inquisitive gelding. The plowhorse laid his ears flat and balked, the gelding obeyed Athren's signals with quivering reluctance, and the mare paced carefully closer as Athren urged her on, finally examining Kestrel from a wary distance. After a moment, the horse relaxed with a dismissive-sounding snort.

"I *thought* Lace would be the best," he said, sliding off the horse's back with an affectionate rub of her chestnut shoulder. "As long as you don't actually try to spook her, I think she'll do well enough." He tossed something sweet-smelling, brown and sticky to Kestrel. "See if she'll take that."

Dubiously, she held the treat out for the mare, who stretched her neck from behind Athren to sniff it with an equally dubious expression.

"For those of us who can't sweet-talk animals directly, bribery usually works pretty well."

"You're sure about that?"

"...eventually." When the mare shifted uneasily and took a step backward, Athren took the treat and stowed it in a saddlebag. "We'll try it again tomorrow, see if we can get her to like you a little better."

She nodded, but doubtfully. Some horses eventually tolerated her, but none she'd ever met would let something that smelled of *predator* on their back. "I'll try. Will we be able to leave tomorrow?"

"If you travel as light as you say, any time after sunup. Meet me at the southern bridge and we'll see what kind of time we can make."

Chapter Twelve

Athren met them just after sunrise, wearing a broad-brimmed hat and a long oilcloth coat. His chestnut mare was loaded with packs and rolls Kestrel couldn't identify, all tied into place with the precision of long practice. Behind her, Otter was grumbling his way through a breakfast of fried, fruit-filled dough from Deeproot's stall, and Fisher was...bouncing. Athren and his scarred chestnut mare both eyed the little girl dubiously, more so when she dropped into fox-shape and spun through three or four circles around Kestrel's feet before popping back upright. "Don't *like* waiting," she explained in answer to Kestrel's perplexed stare.

Athren swung smoothly up to his horse's back, Otter followed more clumsily, and Kestrel handed Fisher up to ride in front of her brother. The little girl scowled for a moment, then settled back with a thoughtful look that hinted at trouble later in the day. As they threaded their way through the early-morning press of cooks, porters, clerks, and merchants, Kestrel kept one hand on Otter's saddle and the other on her sadly depleted belt-pouch.

"So where did you go yesterday?" she asked as they stopped to let a swaying pushcart turn in front of them.

"Docks. I sat and watched the river, mostly. There's some *big* fish down there." He grinned briefly. "I wanted to get a feel for it—some of the people on the fishing fleets say there's huge lizards down south that live in the water, big enough to take down a deer or a cow. None around here, though."

"Lizards." She raised her eyebrows.

"Long as a grown man, they said. They showed me a skin and everything." Enthusiastically, he outlined something suggestive of short legs, spines, and a lot of teeth. "I'd really like to see a live one."

"Bet you would." Curiosity aside, it troubled her that Otter had no form to give him the edge in a fight. She'd had to claw her way out of trouble often enough that she wanted her brother to have the same advantages. "When this is over, maybe we can look down south and find some."

That won her an unexpectedly sweet smile, and he rode in thoughtful silence as they traveled Threeshores' broad lower roads and crossed the southernmost bridge. The traffic thinned around them as they went, leaving them pacing a single caravan that trundled off east along the river as soon as they were on solid ground again.

"All right," Athren said, kneeing his mare into a distance-eating walk as the rumble of the wheels faded away. "I've plotted out our route as best as I could, but I've never had to look for a specific 'blood before. Normally you people look after your own."

"We're *trying*-" Otter began indignantly.

"No insult intended. First time I've had a job like this, and I'm trying to figure out how to...listen...for your people."

Neither of them balked at the odd terminology; beastblood used various terms to describe their perceptions, but there *was* no accurate word for sensing someone or something from a distance. "All right," Kestrel said. "What do you normally do to listen?"

"I can feel 'blood around me—got a pretty good range, actually—and get a good idea of direction and distance. You three, obviously." He waved a hand back behind them. "Mostly greenbloods and stonebloods back at Threeshores, one beastblood about a half-day's walk north, a group of greenbloods up near where the river forks..." He shrugged. "It's easy to tell what and where, but I've never tried 'who'. I'll keep listening as we travel, but I have to save most of my attention for the ride. Once we get closer to the trail you marked, I'll start a more focused search. And—guess it might help me identify your kin from a distance if you tell me something about them. Maybe. I don't think anyone's done something like this before."

"I don't actually know much about the cousins who went missing," Kestrel confessed. "Just their names—Finch, Delver and Tine—and their talents. We're looking for a bird-shifter, someone who works with ferrets and badgers and such, and probably a deer-speaker of some sort. And Mother could work with pretty much any grass-eater."

"Beastblood affect different animals? I thought it was just...all of them, like greenbloods and plants."

"It's complicated," Otter said. "I don't think you could learn enough in a lifetime to be able to cleanse every type of creature."

"So it's in your names?"

"Mostly. We don't know what Fisher's going to take after yet."

He made a thoughtful noise, but said nothing further as they headed further away from the noise and smells of Threeshores. Scrubby trees and hard-packed roads gave slow way to game trails and slender elm trees, and Kestrel felt the returning quiet like cool water on her skin. Athren's scarred little mare kept a wary ear trained on her but made no move to bolt or kick, and Otter's gelding walked steadily behind, apparently enjoying this unexpected herdmate.

When Kestrel took to wolf-form to scout the trail ahead, she heard Otter explaining to Fisher that now would be a good time to practice her listening; the next time she looked back, she saw Fisher in fox-shape perched atop the saddle, ears flicking as she sorted through the forest sounds. These woods weren't dangerous as far as Kestrel could tell, but sharpening her observation was the best way to help the little girl begin to learn her own talents. Kestrel's affinity for predators had been obvious since early childhood, but most beastblood had a period of trial and error to go through before they could identify their strongest skills.

They stopped at midday to rest the horses beside a slow-moving stream choked with algae at its narrowest points. Athren fed each of the horses a hand-sized bar from his packs of concentrated feed, and was leading them toward the stream when Otter snatched the reins.

"Kess," he said in warning, and she froze in her tracks before she could dip her muzzle into the water. "There's nothing alive in there."

She released the wolf-shape. "Blight."

"It's not completely empty," he said, scowling at the lazy flow. "But it's a good distance upstream before there's even minnows in there."

He walked past her and crouched to investigate; behind him, Athren walked the horses farther back from the creek. It looked normal enough to Kestrel—amber-tinted water, weed-grown mud and pebbles at the bottom...but Otter was right, there wasn't a flicker of movement aside from a few placid dimples at the surface. "No bones, either," she reported after a careful look.

Otter stared narrow-eyed at the stream. "Can't be recent, or I'd have felt the creatures dying, but there's no bodies and no smell of sickness. Let me try something." He bent with his hand to the water, and Kestrel grabbed the scruff of his shirt.

"Use a stick or something. Nobody has the time to get eaten."

He pointed to a sodden stick drifting lazily along the current. "Obviously, wood isn't a problem. I want to see if I can get a reaction this way."

"Are all beastblood like this?" Athren inquired mildly.

"Mostly."

"You'd do the same thing, Kess," Otter called over his shoulder.

"*Not* the point."

After a brief not-quite-scuffle, they reached a wordless agreement that Otter would investigate the stream while Kestrel stood ready to haul him back. He crouched to dip a cautious finger in the water, and jerked it back when a slow ripple answered him from somewhere within the mat of algae on the other side. After a moment's thought, he put all his fingers in with an erratic, wriggling motion that would have caught any small predator's interest. This time the algae itself moved, flowing smoothly toward them across the stream.

"*Blight*," Otter said, shaking clinging drops of water off his hand. "Answers *that* question, I guess...my skin's gone numb, too. If that stuff is predatory, it could eat its fill without dinner ever realizing what's happening to it." He scrubbed at his fingers. "Maybe we need that stick now."

Kestrel tossed Otter a flask of spirits from her kit to clean his fingers, while she found a scrap of deadwood and ran it through the mat of algae. It flowed around the stick, creeping upward toward the vibrations of her fingers on the wood, and she dropped the stick with a splash. "All right, I wasn't actually expecting that."

"I wasn't, but I'm not surprised," Athren said, examining the ragged surface of the mat. "The greenbloods back home have been in a twist about something for a few months now. This might be related."

"This is the second time I've run across something like this." Kestrel tramped down the underbrush until she was well upstream of the patch of algae, and took a dubious step into the shallowest part of the stream. She wanted *away* from here. "Plants just don't move fast enough for you to see them. Where is it getting the energy?"

"Magic," suggested Athren, with a withering glance.

She glared right back and splashed across the stream. "Magic doesn't mean that you want something and it happens. Magic is power and it has to come from somewhere. Sunlight doesn't provide enough for something like this, and if it consumed everything in this part of the stream, where is it storing the energy from that? This doesn't obey any of the rules I know."

Athren sighed, and turned into the saddle to rummage through his packs, extricating a wooden disc carved with the same leaf she'd seen on Haila's map. "I admit, I don't like it either. Best I can do, unless you want to take time from looking for your people, is to leave this up where it's easy to see. The next Rider through on circuit will see it and know there's a greenblood needed here."

The simple signal couldn't approach the complexity of Kestrel's worries, but it was all they had. She didn't know how you could begin to carve enough symbols to convey a problem like this. But it would help, at least, and she felt a little relieved as Athren carefully hung the disc up just above the stream and urged his mare across at a brisk, apprehensive trot. Otter followed, with Fisher clinging to the saddlehorn and looking suspiciously down at the water.

Kestrel kept to wolf-form the rest of the day, ears and nose on constant alert for anything out of the ordinary. Between beastblood senses and the horses' night vision, they were able to press on for longer than she was used to before making camp, and they didn't settle for the night until the last glimmers of sunset were fading.

"What has the greenbloods worried, do you know?" she asked as Otter built the fire, with Fisher gravely handing him bits of kindling. The question had pricked at her all afternoon, but not enough to make her willing to give up the wolf's superior senses.

"Not remotely. 'Bloods hardly talk to each other about problems, let alone someone like me. I get bits of rumor here and there, mostly from boat crews or other riders—stories from someone's nephew's cousin's niece about 'bloods going bandit here and there. No two tales the same, but the greenies may know something I don't."

"That's...unnerving." And hard for her to believe; some 'blood had skills that would serve them in combat, yes, but how could they focus when some concentration of taint threatened to overwhelm them?

Athren nodded, his face going tight. "I've wondered a lot why more of you people don't set up a trade for yourselves, but reaving's one I'd rather you didn't try. A stoneblood or a shapeshifter like you could cut through most opposition like a blade through water."

"What stories have you heard?"

"Robbery, mostly; no murder unless the victims tried to stop them. Which victims generally will. One boat captain swears he fought off an ambush with stone-tipped arrows that swerved to follow him, and I *know* that one is possible."

"You do? How?"

"Stoneblood in the family. My brother used to chase me with pebbles without moving a muscle, until I tied a bunch of them to a hornet's nest and hid the strings."

Choking on an unexpected burst of laughter, she asked, "Did it work?"

"Surprisingly well. Better for the apothecary we got our first-aid salve from, though."

"No," Otter said preemptively, brushing soot from his hands as the campfire began to take shape. "Try anything with hornets, and I will replace every single salve you own with bear grease and wait for it to start stinking. I've been hearing some of the same stories, though, from the fishing crews from the west."

"More reason to keep a sharp watch, then. I'll be grateful when we get to the plains and I can keep an eye out from above."

"Where there will be new and interesting emergencies to watch out for," Otter murmured.

Much as she wanted to argue with him, she couldn't.

Chapter Thirteen

The next morning dawned cool and grey, with a damp breeze blowing in that hinted at rain on the way. Smells hung longer and sharper in the humid air, and Kestrel took advantage of the weather to improve their rations. In wolf form, she hung back from her usual far-ranging pace to snap up mice and other small game that the horses flushed out of hiding, detouring occasionally when she caught the sharp smell of wild greens. When a lucky step brought a hare racing across her path, she bolted after it and trotted cheerfully back with the limp body in her jaws. Dinner had just gotten a lot more appealing.

She fell into step beside Otter's gelding and slung the hare up to her brother with a toss of her head.

"I suppose you want me to clean this?"

She signaled an affirmative, making the movement as broad and blatant as possible to properly communicate the unspoken "obviously!"

"So you get all the fun and I get the work."

Athren, who'd been watching Kestrel's side-trips and pounces with amusement, gave him a curious look. "That's fun?"

"Small game is," Kestrel said, releasing the wolf-shape so she could walk in the warm space between the horses. "Deer and barkhide and things like that, not so much—hooves and horns and scales are pretty blighted intimidating when you have to kill something with your teeth. Usually I just stay in the air and scout."

Perched on the front of Otter's saddle, Fisher tipped her head to watch the blackbirds climbing overhead. "Will I be able to do that?"

"Probably. I've never heard of a grown beastblood with only one shape." She'd never heard of one who could shapeshift at

Fisher's age, either, but she didn't know if that was inbred talent or a need for survival.

"So that's just...something you *do* all the time?" Athren asked. "Plan your hunts like a warband, with scouts and everything?"

Kestrel shrugged. "Sometimes. Sometimes I go as a falcon and take whatever birds Otter or one of the cousins flushes up, sometimes we all go for bigger game and I might drive it toward the hunters instead. Mother usually stays behind for big hunts, though; it's uncomfortable for her."

"Because she can speak to deer and such, right? Why doesn't she just call them for you?"

"She could," Kestrel said thoughtfully. "If we were starving, she would. But it's not—not fair, I guess. I wouldn't do it if we wanted...oh, bear pelts or something."

"Merchant thinking on my part, I guess." Athren leaned forward to pat his mare's shoulder, the reins lying loose on her neck. "My Da's a trader, and he's always trying to squeeze extra use out of, well, anything. Which is how my brother and I ended up sliding down four levels of Threeshores stairs in a repurposed rowboat once. Mother was *highly* displeased."

"My mother would've probably demanded her own turn. She used to play tag with me in deer form, when I was little and learning how to shift."

"I remember that. Took you till you were ten to quit tripping over your own paws."

"Cubs have big paws. *I* wasn't the one who hid in a mud puddle all day to get out of scraping hides."

"Mud puddle?" Athren eyed Otter's lanky height, perplexed.

"Tadpole," Kestrel said briefly.

"If you could breathe underwater, you'd have done the same thing."

"I got stuck fishing you out. I'd *rather* have scraped hides." She caught Fisher's speculative expression and added, "And that is not an excuse for you to start finding your way out of chores at home." If they got home, and if they still had family there. If home could ever be what it was again.

Over a late supper of indifferently-seared hare, greens, and wild garlic, Athren pulled a palm-sized miniature of the Riders' carved map out of his saddlebags. It was almost too small to make out its carved features, but Athren traced their journey with a blade of grass. "It's probably two more days to the plains, and if we're lucky, a day or two after that before I'm in range to sense any of your missing 'bloods. Do you have any plans for when you catch up with them?"

"I—no. There's no reason for them to have run in the first place. Somebody really committed might be able to kidnap a beastblood, but not without a much bigger fight than we saw signs of."

"Could a bandit troop make use of a beastblood? Bribery, maybe?"

She bristled. "With *what*? We've got enough work to do, enough to eat, and a safe place to rest." Her belly clenched around a sudden pang of longing for last year's lazy winter evenings—stories at the hearth, games and carving and tanning, offhand meals of stew or jerky when she was hungry—"I mean, most beastblood are good in a fight, but bandits make our life harder just like they do everybody else's. Who'd *help* them?"

Athren spread his hands. "Just asking. I can't rely just on sensing 'bloods, I have to figure out where they're likely to be, or risk losing time that somebody needs to find help. If you say they're not going to turn bandit, I believe you."

Stiffly, she nodded. "Well. We keep food and medicine stashed for emergencies, and all our stores were untouched. Fisher says that Mother was talking to herself, and that's all we know."

"Does she do that normally? Talk to herself?"

Kestrel shook her head.

"Strange." He turned the tiny map over, running a thoughtful finger along its edges. "If something panicked them and they're running to escape, they could be as far away as this..." The grass blade traced an arc close to the northwestern edge of the plains, just shy of the sheer cliff wall that bordered the northern lands. If anyone had been past those cliffs, they'd never returned. "If they're just confused and wandering, hopefully much closer. I've got one of the better ranges in the Riders, so if we're going the right direction, I'll know soon."

"How does that work?"

"Finding 'bloods?" He blinked. "I don't know. How do you know which way is down? I know when I'm looking the right direction, and I know whether I'm getting closer or farther. Usually." He leaned back against his saddle, idly flipping the map once more. "I was actually almost a journeyman with the glasswrights when they noticed that I always knew when my brother was coming to visit, and after that, nothing would do but that I trained with the Riders instead."

"Your idea?" Otter's eyes narrowed thoughtfully.

"More or less." The uneasy shift of his shoulders wasn't quite a shrug. "I liked making glasswork, but I like seeing new things—anything. Everything, really. And if Mother couldn't have two stoneblood sons, she'd settle for a stoneblood and a Rider instead of some lowly craftsman that nobody notices working." He returned the map to its place with exaggerated care. "Besides, I'm good with horses."

"You can have 'em," Kestrel muttered. In the flickering firelight, she thought she saw Otter's gelding laying its ears back at her.

"I don't know, I'd still like to see if I could get Lace to carry you."

Kestrel snorted. "Horses get a whiff of me and decide that every predator in the land is sitting there staring at them. I don't think even your horse is going to put up with having me in prime biting position."

"Give her time. She's had to learn plenty of strange things already."

"Like what?"

"Oh, the time I had to fix a footbridge with strangleweed—it was a narrow bridge, I just had to be quick with a machete—or the time I had to haul a trellis into place for a gaggle of greenbloods that were trying to separate slumbervine from *some* useful plant or other that they kept trying to explain to me..." He went on with more half-explained stories of a life on the move, and Kestrel countered him with some of her more interesting (or terrifying) encounters. Fisher listened intently, but Otter's expression gradually closed in on itself until Kestrel noticed it and turned the conversation back to observations he could share. She didn't think she did it *well*, but her brother seemed to appreciate the effort.

Athren took first watch that night, and she dozed by the fire until her turn came; they'd already agreed to save Kestrel's sharper senses for the darkest part of the night. As he passed her, he held out a hand that almost brushed her arm. "I can't promise we'll find your people. But I'll use every trick I know to get you close."

"Thanks."

Chapter Fourteen

The forest thinned around them over the next few days of travel, changing gradually from towering hardwoods to weedy pines and underbrush. The smaller hunters whose thoughts Kestrel sensed were wary, vaguely aware of thinning prey and an increasing number of carnivorous plants. Kestrel dug up young stranglevines in passing, keeping a careful eye out for any plants she didn't recognize and wishing for a greenblood's knowledge.

Eventually, she realized they were being followed. A whiff of distant smoke, fainter and colder than their last campfire could account for, put her on alert but could have been hunters or a far-off lightning strike. But when a gusty breeze brought her the scent of an unfamiliar horse and something not quite human, she broke off from her scouting and circled back to find Otter. The horses snorted in surprise when she left the underbrush, but she ignored the mare's warning stomp and trotted down the path toward her brother.

He straightened in the saddle and reined to a halt. "What's wrong?"

Trouble behind, she signaled. *Stay alert.*

"You're going to look into it?"

Yes.

"And probably pick a fight with it."

She looked evasively aside.

"*Kess.*"

She dropped her jaw in a canine grin and leaped, reaching the trees in a blur of feathers as she took to her namesake form. Brown-feathered and hardly bigger than a dove, a kestrel was unlikely to attract attention, and despite Otter's teasing, she had no intention of being noticed.

She covered their backtrail in short flights from tree to tree, searching the pines around her for any sign of danger. When the trees thickened, she went back to marten-shape and followed her nose. Unreliable it might be, but the wind brought her more information than she could get peering through the mass of leaves and vines around her.

Claws gripping the flaking red bark beneath her, she trotted from one branch to another, testing the breeze at every step. Pine sap dulled with the approach of autumn, sweet, musty smells from the leaves and sandy dryness from the red soil below her, hours-old traces of fox and mouse and bird—and *there*, a wash of sweet-toned grazer smell, with a clean-scrubbed overtone that spoke of human care. Horse-scent for sure; large, in good condition, and not one she knew. A faint, unintelligible murmur, possibly a man's voice or the squeaking of leather tack, made her prick up her ears and swerve toward the distant sound.

Close up, the smell resolved itself into a mild mixture of grain, horsehide, and leather; she crouched lower on her branch as the horse and rider passed beneath her. The horse was a tall, well-fed gelding, carefully tacked and carrying a set of travelers' rolls and packs on his saddle. And the rider—stoneblood to his core, with flinty-smooth skin and a trace of mottling around the knuckles like inclusions in granite. He was wrapped in an oilcloth coat like Athren's, so she couldn't get a good idea of his appearance, but the dusty-dry note to his scent told her well enough what he was.

She climbed noiselessly down from her tree, intending to take a look for weapons or armor before rejoining Otter to work out their next decision. A moment after her paws touched the ground, the rider stiffened, and a jagged pebble rose up from the trail and shot over her head.

She flung herself sideways, rolled, and came up as a wolf, leaping backward to avoid another, larger stone. The horse squealed, bucked, and bolted, leaving his rider in a momentary heap on the ground, but the stoneblood was picking himself up before Kestrel could react. Without a glance after the fleeing horse, he scrabbled in a pouch at his waist and came out with a handful of stones, polished smooth and round like sling bullets. A gesture, and they rose to circle his hand.

Kestrel darted for the other side of the path, where the dense underbrush might hide her. One of the polished stones whistled after her, arcing in its path to follow her as she swerved. She'd fought off animals in plenty, and very occasionally human bandits, but never another 'blood. Athren's rumors flooded back into her mind. Fight and flight were equally unappealing, but she refused to lead any danger back to her family.

Teeth bared, she circled through the sheltering brush and lunged, head snaking low to slash at the 'blood's unprotected legs. He pivoted enough to protect the great vein she'd been aiming for, but she ripped through breeches and opened the side of his knee instead. His stones flew wide in the shock of the moment, but as Kestrel whirled to leap again, a carpet of dirt and tiny pebbles rose to pelt her like a hailstorm, stinging the skin beneath her fur and leaving her blinking and half-blind in the dust. She lifted her head, the wolf's streamlined features replaced by a bear's blunt muzzle and heavy fur, and charged with a roar.

For just a moment, she saw the stoneblood blink, before he took a step back and sliced one hand firmly upward. The earth around them erupted into a duststorm, and from somewhere in the haze she heard a shrill, metallic whistle, Head down, she lumbered forward and swatted with outstretched claws. She could probably get to safety in bird-shape, but reinforcements would be bad, bad news for Fisher and Otter-

Pain flashed along her pads as dirt began to rise and harden around her feet. She snarled, pulled her paws free, and spun to leap for the trees in cat-shape. Ears flat and tail lashing, she flowed along the branches to slash down at the stoneblood's neck and shoulders.

She could hear approaching hoofbeats, but couldn't make out their direction in the haze. If he'd summoned reinforcements...

A rock aimed for her eyes took her in the shoulder, leaving a bone-deep bruise. She dropped from the tree, touched down, and leaped for another across the trail, pivoting on its trunk to keep her paws off the ground and away from the stoneblood's control. Claws flexing, she drove straight for her opponent, hoping for a pinning strike to knock him off-balance.

"Hands *off!*" The shout came from up the trail and shocked both of them into an instant of stillness before Kestrel scrambled for her tree again. Athren cantered down the path, glaring at Kestrel and the strange stoneblood impartially.

Behind him, Otter slowed to a halt, crossbow cocked and Fisher clinging behind him. "Kess?"

She signaled *Safe* at him but kept her gaze fixed on Athren, her ears tipped warily back. When the Rider looked up at her, she slitted her eyes and lifted her chin in a convince-me gesture.

Athren let out an explosive sigh with more than a hint of a growl in it. "That," he said, indicating the bleeding stoneblood, "is my big brother." He turned to the stoneblood with exaggerated patience and a jerk of his hand toward Kestrel. "*That* is my client. And that-" he finished with a wave toward the trampled brush in front of him. "*Was* my horse, who you apparently decided to borrow, and who is now on his way back to Threeshores as fast as his hooves can take him."

Kestrel flicked her tail, unconvinced.

Athren scrubbed both hands over his face. "I am going to go catch my horse before something eats him. You are going to stay here and none of you are going to try to kill anyone else. All right? All right." He turned his mare neatly around on the narrow path and trotted off after the stoneblood's fleeing horse.

"Well," Otter said. After a dubious moment, he tentatively uncocked his crossbow. The stoneblood returned his bullets to their pouch with broad, can't-miss gestures and gave Kestrel an expectant look; she left the cat-form behind but stayed on her branch. Fisher eyed the strange stoneblood up and down, put her nose in the air, and turned into a fox. "This isn't confusing at *all*."

Chapter Fifteen

By the time Athren returned, they had established a wary truce. Still atop her branch, Kestrel was carefully rubbing arnica salve into her bruised shoulder, and had unbent enough to give the stoneblood a bandage or two (with a mental promise to rip them right back off again if she didn't like Athren's explanation). Otter was keeping an uneasy eye on the trail and the stoneblood was...waiting, as still as any rock. His soot-grey eyes were narrowed in thought as he watched the three beastblood, but he remained otherwise expressionless until he finally shifted his weight and looked up at Kestrel.

"So. I'm sorry I tried to hurt you."

"Likewise." She considered the situation. "Probably."

"*Kess,*" Otter hissed.

She huffed in annoyance—at herself, mostly; that had been too hostile by far, with the rush of battle still bubbling through her. "Look, if Athren vouches for you, I *am* sorry. We've been hearing some bad things lately, and when I saw you following our trail, I assumed you were an enemy."

"Same here. And whatever you've heard, there's likely more and worse out there."

She raised her eyebrows. "Like what?"

"Reliable stories of 'blood going bandit. I've seen some of the evidence myself. Seems to be worse among beastblood—no offense—so when Athren told me he had a couple of you wanting him to guide you out on the plains somewhere, I got concerned."

"And then you threw rocks at her head." Bedraggled but leading the runaway horse, Athren walked his weary mare slowly up to them. "You realize, there are middle steps between noticing someone's there and trying to kill them."

"She *was* sneaking up on me," the stoneblood pointed out mildly.

"I scout. It's my job to sneak." Kestrel swung her legs and dropped down to the ground. "Athren, who is he, why is he here, and is he going to make a habit of throwing rocks at me?"

"My brother Shale, I don't know why he's here, and you'll have to ask him about the rocks." Athren slid off his mare and bent to run his hand over the retrieved gelding's legs and hooves. "Preferably while we're moving."

"I told her, I was worried." Shale shrugged out of his coat and lowered his head to peer at Athren's examination. "Did I let him get hurt?"

"No. Just a few light scratches. And I can do my job."

He shrugged uneasily. "Normally, yes. But the rumors are getting worse and scarier. Most of the family sticks around Threeshores where it's safe, but with you—I worried. Da worried. And Mother-"

"Didn't." Athren straightened abruptly.

There was a hesitation. "No."

"We're a little more than a year apart," Shale explained as he rode alongside Otter. Kestrel's shoulder still ached from the flying stone, leaving her utterly uninterested in anything that required four legs or wings, so she was walking just ahead of the two geldings and relying on Fisher's nose for advance information. The trail was knobbly with pine roots and pebbles, but at least the trees were thinning and would give her room to fly when she healed. "I started linking to the stone early and Athren went for a Rider, but we kept touch as often as we could. I shadow him sometimes—although usually he knows about it—so he can teach me more trail skills than most stoneblood know, and I can teach him whatever I learn while I'm working."

"Learn how?"

He shrugged. "When you feel the stone, you know what it knows. Athren likes knowing—well, pretty much everything—so when I find out something interesting, I tell him."

"Except for not telling him you were on his trail."

"Figured I'd let him know eventually. I can usually take care of myself, and the stone tells me when there's danger nearby. And after the stuff I saw at midsummer, I didn't want to worry him.

"What did you see?" Kestrel's eyes narrowed, in lieu of the lashing tail she didn't have at the moment.

"'Saw' isn't quite right, I guess. Somebody raised a fortress out to the southwest, and I felt it go up. Had to be stoneblood work, but it was nobody I knew, and it didn't feel right. So I went to get a closer look." He hesitated. "I'm glad I didn't look too close. There were mostly bandits, but a few 'bloods in there, different types as far as I could tell. They just—didn't *move* right. The only look I got with my own eyes, they seemed normal, but...well. Stone floors and all that, I could feel them walking and they didn't walk right. Can't explain it better than that, and I cleared out in case it was some sort of contagion."

Some kind of pattern tugged at her mind, but piecing it together felt like trying to scent-track through snow. "I haven't seen anything particularly unusual, but I spend most of my time with animals and they don't exactly gossip."

"And you might not see what's going on because animals can run away when something hurts them."

"Hurts?"

"Just because it's not what you call living doesn't mean it doesn't react. Whoever raised that fortress had power but not skill, and it...hurt."

Kestrel shook her head. "Everything I ran across before midsummer was—not easy, I guess, but normal. After, I ran into a corn crop out of control and then whatever happened at home. Nothing's related as far as I can see."

"Nor me, but the greenbloods are antsy and you've run across a couple instances of plants acting unusually. I can't help thinking they're connected."

"Doubt it. I don't see many carnivorous plants, but there's still enough that everybody has to learn how to deal with them. And bandits...happen sometimes, and even beastblood can't always fight them off."

"Do you really think bandits took your family?"

She had no answer.

She'd expected that Shale's presence would make travel more awkward, but he pulled his weight at their campsites as they left the forests behind for patchy woodlands and growing expanses of grass. Having a fourth adult around meant that one of them could get a full night's rest each time they camped, and he had enough experience riding that Athren could leave the pathfinding to his brother and concentrate on searching instead. For all the good it was doing. Even hawk's eyes hadn't found any traces of human passage here, and any scent trail was long gone. Kestrel hadn't really expected success this early, but that hadn't stopped her hoping.

"Tell me about your family," Athren said as they made camp at the edge of the plains. "The more I know, the more I'll have to listen for and the better chance we'll have."

"That's harder than it sounds," she said after a moment's thought, hanging back at a cautious distance while Athren hobbled the horses. His little mare pricked longing ears toward the sweet, damp scent of prairie grasses from the west, but accepted his offering of a feed bar with reasonable grace. "The cousins come and go, and Mother *never* goes—went--" It was surprisingly hard, creating an accurate image of someone who'd always been there. "She makes most of our medicines, she was teaching me...she's better at making things than patrolling, so whenever any of us came in we'd just tell her about things she needed to look into. She thinks it's important for us to have a safe place to rest when we're not working—our house has been there a long time, but she's the one who arranged for storage and defenses and whatnot."

Athren finished untacking the horses and began to rub them down; wordlessly, Kestrel started shifting saddles and packs toward the rest of their gear, since the horses wouldn't let her touch them. "That's a start. Who else?"

"The three I told you about, but I barely know them. Crane never made it away, and if anyone else showed up while I was gone, I didn't find any trace of them. People come and go, but usually home's mostly empty until late fall or winter. I wish we'd had some way to leave word for anyone who's come home since."

"I know what you mean. We spend a lot of our apprentice time learning different signals and how to arrange them, like that sign I left for the greenbloods, but there's only so many you can carry and only so many arrangements. And I don't think anybody's come up with a carving for 'family missing under strange circumstances, send help'." He finished grooming the mare, released her to grace with a pat, and took his brush to Otter's gelding. "Stoneblood can make tokens to tell us that we're needed back at the hall, but not why or when. 'Come home' is all you can say, not 'come home right rotting *now'* or 'take your time'."

"*Is* that home? The Rider's hall?"

He stared off over the gelding's shoulder. "The stables, maybe. I like horses."

"Somebody has to," she muttered mutinously.

"I got packed off to the glassblowers when the family figured out I'd never have any real connection to the stone. Shale would come to visit me, and when they noticed I always knew when he was coming—well, that was good enough for the Riders. It's important work, and I like seeing new places."

"But?"

"But." He went to tend Shale's horse, shoulders pulled in on themselves like a cat's in hostile territory. Shale took a look at his brother and stepped aside, digging a flat, oval brush out of his saddlebag and tossing it to Athren. "I do good work, though, and I can pass on some of what I do to Shale so he's not completely at a loss outside of Threeshores. My da is from a merchant family, and my mother is stoneblood, and neither of them would make it a half-day away from home without bolting for safety."

She tilted her head, intrigued. "Usually beastblood only marry other beastblood. Farmers, sometimes, but that's the only other people we ever *see* for long."

Athren shrugged. "That's cities for you, lots more people mixing around. I wish I could spend more time there. There used to be more than just Threeshores and a bunch of nameless trading posts, but Northkeep emptied out from plague and Farwatch just...died."

"How does a city die?"

Shale swallowed. "Farwatch died because the stoneblood thought it was safe and it wasn't. It's the reason we mostly live in cities now. The original plan was to build a place that could serve as a fortress, then move on and start another. By the time we realized something was wrong, there weren't enough stoneblood to contain it."

"That was a city? I've seen it from the air, but I thought it was just...rocks. Like those thin walls that you find sometimes."

"Those may be stoneblood work too, for all I know. I've never been able to go deep enough to find out."

"So what happened to destroy it?"

"We don't really know. Still. Farwatch was raised almost in the center of the plains—the original builders wanted a vantage point where they could gather 'bloods and watch out for trouble—but stone from that area has always been unstable. Angry. Little things started happening after a few years, walls shearing or railings breaking away, but it got worse and faster. People started to run eventually, when the deaths got too many to be ignored, but the stoneblood there weren't able to protect them all. The walls started breaking into shards or impaling people who came near, the floors absorbed anyone who stood still for too long...if you're stoneblood, you can still feel it in the rocks that came from there. We keep a few cached near every major settlement so none of us ever forget."

Kestrel rubbed the back of her arms; personally, if she had to die, she'd rather let something eat her and have her body be of some use. Otter just frowned. "You sound like you think it's your fault."

"I don't think that. Feeling's another matter."

Kestrel snorted. "You weren't even alive, what's to feel about it?"

"Memory is tricky for stonebloods. If I listen long enough to a bit of stone, I can learn what happened around it, but it's more like being there than hearing a story. Everyone who tried to save Farwatch knew it was their fault, so..." He shrugged. "So do I."

"Me, I'd rather just listen to the stories," Kestrel said. "Older beastblood tell them to teach their apprentices, then we all trade the good ones wherever we end up for the winter."

Shale considered the idea. "We don't really have apprentices. Stoneblood can send thoughts and memories into rock if it's accustomed to them—that's why most of us wear a stone bracelet or amulet—and the rest of us can learn from that even after they're dead."

"And their brothers think it's creepy," Athren muttered.

"Doesn't matter if it's creepy, as long as it works."

"Ghost teachers? Sounds like it'd make a good hearthtale."

"It's not a ghost, just...a way to pass things on. Stone can hold information. Even emotion if the feelings are strong enough."

"He used to use pebbles to sneak messages to me at the glasswright's," Athren said with a reminiscent grin. "Made it a lot easier to rearrange chores so I could slip out and go fishing instead."

Otter nodded solemnly. "Fish is always better if you're not supposed to be catching it." Fisher giggled.

"I just wonder what would happen if you could share messages like that with everybody, whether they're related or not. Or *dead* or not. If you could get more 'bloods and artificers, or 'bloods and farmers, combining talents instead of using them to pull each other out of trouble." He ran the currycomb in wide gestures over the gelding's barrel. "Creating something instead of just scrambling to make it through the next emergency. And away from the trade ports, there doesn't seem to be time to do anything *but* survive."

"It's dangerous out in the wilds." She dragged one of the saddles back over and dropped it to the ground to use as a backrest. "Farmers wouldn't be able to feed themselves, let alone have anything to trade, without beastbloods and greenbloods clearing them some breathing room."

"I *know* that." He waved the currycomb in frustration, and the gelding snorted and eyed him suspiciously. "But don't you ever wonder what you could do if you didn't have to make that room?"

"Not really." There was always more that needed tending, and it was all but impossible to ignore a taint that you could feel.

He shook his head. "I got raised stoneblood. Everybody thought I'd be out reinforcing trails or shaping buildings or–all that stuff. When it didn't happen, I started wondering what else it was good for. If you had a stoneblood glasswright or blacksmith, what could they make? Or if a greenblood had time and peace to improve crops instead of just keeping them quiescent, or, or one of your people could try healing humans as well as beasts?"

She sucked in a sudden breath, trying to smooth bristling fur that wasn't actually there. "That would be—ugly."

He blinked, distracted from his tale-spinning. "How?"

"If you know something well enough to cleanse it, you can control it if you want. Your brother can move rocks around. I could have a pack of wolves marching in step if I chose to. Nobody should have the option to do that to *people*."

He frowned in thought. "I guess you're right about that. But...no more wasting sickness, no killing cough in the winter...I'd love to see that."

"Me too. But you're likelier to see it from the apothecaries than the beastblood."

"Maybe so." He rubbed the grey gelding's forehead, and was rewarded with an affectionate nudge that left him slightly staggered and with a trail of short white hairs down his shirt front.

Still, the idea lingered. Kestrel had no desire—or time—to practice human medicine, but expanding her skills by working with an apothecary was oddly tempting. She was all concentration as she stalked rabbits for that night's dinner, but turned the idea over in her thoughts as she drifted to sleep afte rher watch.

When she woke, Athren was pacing through the campsite, glancing westward with every few steps. "Kestrel. I think I've found something."

Chapter Sixteen

"Three beastblood, two men and one woman. Young and traveling slowly." Athren handed his brother an implausible tangle of bridles, packs, and unidentifiable straps and nodded toward the horses with an absent, "Take care of that, would you?" He turned back to Kestrel. "They don't seem to be in trouble, more...sleepy...than anything else, but I can't tell much more from this distance."

"Sleepy" she could understand, this soon after sunrise. But Kestrel couldn't imagine any situation where her kin *weren't* in trouble, not after the way she and Otter had found their home. "How soon can we reach them?" She bundled up her bedroll in tight, hurried movements and set it aside to be strapped onto Otter's gelding.

"This evening, unless they're trying to shed pursuit for some reason. But we're not going to hurt the horses trying to catch up. Walk and trot will get us there and save their strength in case we need to run."

Kestrel let out a frustrated breath. Athren had training and experience on his side, but they were so *close*-! "I'll fly ahead and scout. If I'm high enough, I can see well ahead of us and still stay in contact."

He eyed her up and down. "Will your shoulder take that?"

"It'll have to."

His eyebrows quirked dubiously, but he didn't try to talk her down. "All right. If you don't see anything, stay on track with us; I can sense their direction pretty clearly now."

She nodded. "Otter can call me down if you need me quickly. Otherwise, I'll be back if I learn anything new." She exchanged a quick, fierce squeeze of hands with Otter, ran a soothing hand over Fisher's back, and took in a calming breath before changing shape to flap heavily upward. Her shoulder twinged with every wingbeat, but the falcon's endurance would serve her best when she got to scouting height.

She lifted herself laboriously through the cool morning air, casting about for the beginnings of a thermal to lift her. Lingering warmth from their campfire and the bare earth around it gave her a little of the lift she needed, and she circled it until a rising breeze gave her something to climb against. Razor-sharp shadows from grass and insects faded and blurred as she rose, stretching her raptor's vision to its limit. To the west, at the far edge of her sight, she saw a faint line that might be crushed grass and angled toward it, grudging every moment she spent working for height.

With little smell and no sound but the rush of the wind around her, sight filled her whole world. On the ground, her family and the others had cleared camp and were preparing to ride out; Fisher stood looking up with her eyes shaded until Otter gently scooped her into the saddle and mounted behind her. They looked tiny as mice in the falcon's wide-angled vision, almost lost in the shadows of clouds and wind-driven waves in the grass, and Kestrel relaxed some of her westward focus to keep an eye on the figures below her.

The air around her warmed as the morning wore on, an occasional thermal providing lift without straining her shoulder further. At this height, she couldn't make out expressions, but the set of Athren's shoulders was confident as he kept the horses moving at a steady trot. She could feel a barkhide lurking nearby, but the ambush predator was sated and sleepy, and barely flicked an ear at the vibrations from the passing travelers. Far away, a subtle shift in the grasses and a sense of *sunny morning strong pack nose to the wind* marked a group of the great plains wolves; she turned their path with a subtle pulse of power before they could catch the scent of horses on the wind.

A little further west, she broke off from her climb to focus on the distorted pattern in the grass ahead. Definitely crushed, but by something larger than a human; her missing kin might well be riding, though that didn't tell her why they would be riding *away*.

Reluctantly, she dropped a few dozen manlengths for a closer look. The grasses below came almost to her shoulder in human form, but these were leaning at an angle from the passage of something large. Matted roots and dry soil didn't leave much for her to track with, but she thought she saw partial crescent-shapes here and there along the trail.

She tipped her wings for a long, descending flight along the trail until she was skimming just above the grasses, then dropped and hit the ground in the familiar brindled wolf-shape. She shook her head in a moment's disorientation at the returning flood of smell and sound after the remote stillness of the sky. Rustling grass, tiny sounds from mice and insects, the distant shriek of some unlucky rabbit...smells were just as overwhelming, but after a pause to collect herself she was able to focus on the damp green smell of broken grass.

By the time she'd trotted a few lengths along the trail, she was no longer in any doubt. Three horses whose scent she knew in passing, the leather-and-oil smell of well-used tacks, and a lingering human scent with a wilder beastblood tang. Sheer relief made her stand lock-kneed for a moment with her head and tail hanging loose; at least some of the missing 'bloods were still *alive*, and maybe some of the mysteries gnawing at her would be solved.

Ears pricked hopefully, she angled away from the beastbloods' trail and toward the cool scent of water on the breeze. Water meant trees, and trees would keep her from another struggle for altitude like this morning's. The wolf's size and sleek coat let her weave her way through the towering grass at the roots, where the stems were easy to push through, and it didn't take long for her to reach a copse of trees surrounding a thread-thin stream.

She splashed across the stream and glared at the young barkhide hidden in the trees. A snarl and mental projection of *bigger hunter than you* left the armored predator sulking under its trunk, and Kestrel shifted into human form just long enough to clamber up the sturdiest of the trees around her.

Back in the falcon's shape, she hopped down the branch until it was clear of twigs, spread her wings, and swooped out onto an updraft. Her shoulder protested, but the lift from the thermal was enough to get her back to a useful height. A glance downward showed her Otter and the rest still on track. She hesitated for a moment, torn between information for her brother and the need to know *more*. After so long, she wouldn't believe they'd caught up to the missing beastblood until she could see and smell them in front of her.

The sight-trail grew fresher as she flew, and when the sun began to lower she caught her first glimpse of three mounted figures. Mere dots at first, they came into clearer focus as she traded height for speed as only a falcon could. She recognized one immediately: Delver, whose affinity with badgers and other burrowers gave her *some* reason to be out on the plains. The others came back to her after a moment's thought: broad-built Tine and Finch with his tangle of gold-tinged hair. They rode easily but far too casually, with none of the wariness that any 'blood learned in childhood. No one was watching for danger, none of them had noticed her approach, and their very presence was...wrong, a trio of tight, contained little eddies instead of the river-strong sensation she was used to.

She coasted a few lengths over their heads, dove, and pivoted down to the ground. "Delver! Are you all right?"

"I'm perfectly fine." The other beastblood, a young woman with brown eyes and a sleek dark braid, reined to a stop and nodded at her with an expression of pleasant neutrality. The reins lay easily in her thick-nailed hands, even when her horse stamped and shifted restlessly at Kestrel's presence. "Why wouldn't I be?"

"You *disappeared*. What happened? Have you seen Roe?"

"I don't know. I haven't seen anybody." She glanced after Finch and Tine, who had kept moving at that same easy walk.

Neither of them had so much as paused at Kestrel's sudden appearance.

"What happened?" Her fingers curved into claw-shapes, wanting to swat something in sheer frustration. "Otter and I came home and it was empty. We thought there had been some kind of attack."

"No. We needed to go."

"Go where?" She felt a purely human chill coil in her belly. Whatever was wrong, it was nothing predator's instincts could recognize, but the other woman was as lost as she'd ever been. Delver didn't look or smell sick, but no beastblood born had ever been that placid.

"I don't know. I need to go there." She kneed her horse into a walk. Kestrel kept pace at a cautious distance.

"Go wh-" Kestrel broke off in a frustrated growl. "Look, Mother's still missing, home is half-destroyed or worse, I've got a fosterling in need of *real* care, and Otter and I have tracked the three of you halfway across the country. What exactly is going on?"

"Why should I tell you?" Delver blinked, perplexed. "Who are you anyway?"

Chapter Seventeen

"Blight it, Delver, I'm Kestrel and you know it!" She bared her teeth for a frustrated instant.

"You're not important. I have to go." Delver turned her horse away.

Kestrel snarled, an audible ripple of sound this time and not just a show of useless human teeth. "Rot me if you do."

She snatched the horse's reins. The horse snapped at Kestrel and reared, the trailing reins leaving a long weal across her palm as it plunged away. Delver tumbled unceremoniously to the ground, and without thinking Kestrel darted forward to help her up.

"No! I have to *go!*" Delver ducked away and sliced at Kestrel's forearm with broad, blunt claws, leaving a set of bloody furrows behind. Hand still outstretched, Kestrel grabbed for the badger's scruff. The other beastblood snapped at her, hunched closer to the ground, and scrambled out of reach.

If that's how you want to do this... Kestrel shook herself and dropped into bear-form, loping forward to catch up with the fleeing Delver. Carefully, she rolled the badger off her feet with the swipe of a canteen-sized paw. Delver scrabbled to her feet with a growl rumbling in her throat, spun ponderously in place, and shrank abruptly into something that dashed through Kestrel's paws in a streak of countershaded brown fur. Kestrel's reflexive snap caught nothing but a musky whiff of weasel-scent.

Trading toughness for agility, Kestrel whirled and snapped again as a mountain cat, trying for a mouthful of fur that would immobilize the other beastblood without hurting her. She yowled a single attack cry in hopes that Otter would hear it, but that was all she had time for; any digger was at an advantage with this much cover, and whatever was wrong with Delver, she'd lost none of her human intelligence.

In human form, she managed to snatch the weasel's hind leg before it could disappear among the tangled grasses, but instead of clawing her as Kestrel had expected, Delver whipped around and used three paws to pry the fourth loose. Kestrel vaulted upward in a blur of feathers and dropped down again with talons outstretched; they closed loosely around the weasel's body, and she tried to lift off. Delver shifted shape again, the stocky badger-body and thick fur too much for any talons, and rolled to shake her off.

For an instant, she looked confused. She shook her shaggy head, glanced around, then saw Kestrel and headed for open ground. Kestrel took off again to follow her, a breath behind when Delver burst into a hare's form and fled.

Kestrel dropped to the ground as a wolf and raced after her with ears flat to her skull, driving herself with all the speed she could muster. At the very least, Delver was a thread in the tangle of mysteries that surrounded her, and *blight* if she'd lose it now. She tumbled sideways when she swerved after a sudden hairpin turn from Delver, but rolled back to her feet and *sprinted*, hoping to beat the other beastblood to a suspicious shadow on the ground ahead of them. If that was a burrow, she'd never sort this out--

She lunged, and swatted Delver away with a sideways sweep of her muzzle as they reached the burrow entrance. The hare tumbled end-over-end, landing as something low, lean and stripey that scrabbled for momentum—then dug its paws in and took a cautious step backward, staring up at Kestrel. Another step back, and the ferret hunkered down against the earth and tilted her head.

Safe? The signal came slowly, hard to read past the ferret's thick fur and heaving sides. *No fight.*

Trying hard to look unthreatening, Kestrel sat down and returned to her human form, holding her hands loosely at her sides. "It's not remotely safe here. But I can watch your back, if you're done trying to run away from me."

The ferret blinked at her, bright eyes dazed and distant. After a moment, she shivered, stretched, and returned to her human form, as much the worse for their long chase as Kestrel was. Her hands were scuffed and scratched, and one or two of Kestrel's swipes were probably going to bruise spectacularly.

"...Kestrel." Delver scrubbed at a streak of dirt along one forearm. "What on all the stones were you *doing?*"

"You don't remember?"

She drew an indignant breath. "No, I d...I don't," she finished quietly. "Why don't I?"

"You and the others have been missing for almost a month now." The two of them had limped along their backtrail to meet Otter and the others halfway, where they'd set up the bare bones of a camp while Otter scolded Kestrel roundly for pursuing the missing beastblood without informing the rest of them. Now Delver was sitting with her back against a saddle, sipping her way dubiously through a dose of tonic while Otter's gelding enjoyed the unplanned rest. "We don't know how, much less why—Mother sent us off on an errand, and when we got back, home was just...empty."

"Whatever it was, it looked sudden," Otter said. "But no blood, and nothing valuable missing except people."

Delver finished the tonic with a mute grimace for the bitter taste; wordlessly, Shale handed her a full canteen. "It's hard to remember back that far--"

"Less than a month?" Athren cut in, and Kestrel and Otter both shot him a quelling look.

"It feels like longer. Or not like anything. Like being underwater." Delver twined her braid thoughtfully around one hand, wincing when it caught on torn skin. "Someone called, I opened the door, and then...then I just needed to go. So I took one of the horses and started riding."

"Riding where?"

"Where he—she? *Somebody* wanted me." Delver swallowed. "It's not clear."

Fisher looked her up and down, dropped the grass stems she'd been playing with, and clambered over the saddle to sit next to Delver. The contact seemed to comfort the older beastblood, and some of the strained lines around her eyes eased. "Whatever it was, I wanted to go. Felt like someone would be happy to see me."

"But go where?" Kestrel pressed. "You were riding west—Finch and Tine still are, as far as I know. What's to the west?"

Her shoulders pulled unhappily inward. "Blight if I know. There was no hurry, but no stopping either. Ride till you're tired, sleep till you wake, and do it again. And again. I don't remember how many times."

Otter gave her a narrow-eyed look; Kestrel could all but see his mind racing behind the calm expression. "Kess said she found all three of you close together. Were you riding *with* them, or just sort of in the same direction?"

"Same direction. When Kestrel stopped me, I didn't think to call either of them for help."

"What did you think?"

"I was...frustrated?" She looked over to Kestrel. "You wouldn't stop bothering me and I had someplace to go. Then my horse threw me and I thought that if I could just get underground, I could wait you out and get on my way again."

Kestrel frowned. "Yes, but something got you thinking again."

"I couldn't tell you what. I kept having to change to dodge you—*would* you really have bitten me?"

"No, but I was about ready to swat you all the way back home."

Delver snorted with reluctant laughter. "Just remember *I* can't fly. After—I guess after the third or fourth time I changed, I wondered why you were chasing me, and the time after that I remembered who you were and that we shouldn't be fighting. But I still didn't know why."

"Neither do I. I'd almost think it was some form of corruption." Delver recoiled, and Kestrel continued with a hastily muttered apology. "Except I've never heard of a corrupted human, or of a taint clearing away without some sort of intervention. And I don't think chasing you all over the place counts as intervention."

"Good. Because I'd rather not do it again."

Kestrel nodded in heartfelt agreement.

Late that afternoon, while Delver rested and Athren took advantage of the opportunity to pamper the horses, Otter drew Kestrel aside under the pretense of repacking her medicine kit. "So what do you think?"

"I think we don't know a rotting thing more than we did this morning."

"We *know* more, we just can't make sense of it yet. And Delver's tired out, not talked out—we may be able to piece something together later tonight."

She nodded, carefully strapping bottles back into place to give her hands something to do.

"It's one of our people back safe, at least."

"It is. I just wish-" She squeezed her eyes shut.

Otter's arm around her shoulders came as a surprise. "Me too. Be nice to just find everybody, get home safe, and stop worrying about anything except turning into a fish. Which all of a sudden looks like a way smaller problem than it used to be. But this is too big to fix all at once."

"Or at all, the way things are going. We lost Finch and Tine again-"

"Stop that. We know where they're going now."

"Maybe. It sounds like repeated shifting brought Delver back—not that I know how—I might be able to maneuver Tine into something like that, but Finch is a bird-shifter and I can't think of a way to corner him."

Otter glanced away, looking somber for a moment before he forced himself back into his expression of determined good cheer. Kestrel raised her eyebrows at him. "And?"

"...and I need you to be careful, Kess."

"That's a benefit of being connected to predators, at least. There's not much out there that can really hurt me if I'm watching for it."

He scowled. "What if you can't watch out? Watching didn't help Delver."

"What do you mean?"

"I don't *know* what I mean! Something feels wrong. Poisonous. We can fight off humans and animals, we're generally strong enough to push through wounds and diseases and the like, but whatever happened to Delver and the rest was just...thinking."

"So's half of what we do with-"

The hair on her neck and arms lifted as the parallels arranged themselves in her mind. She could convince a rampaging bear or a stalking fox to obey her with a thought, could have a dozen wolves for a bodyguard if she cared to use her power that way. But just because *she'd* never tried it... "Otter. What if there's someone out there that can control *us*?"

His eyes widened. "Blight."

She saw Delver to sleep after an anxious dinner around the campfire, contributing her bedroll when the younger beastblood tried to improvise a bed out of one of their ground covers. Otter glared at her, but Kestrel ignored him; she was comfortable sleeping in beast-form or out of it, and a wolf's thick coat was proof against more than a summer night on the prairie.

She dozed close to the fire until her turn came for watch, then rose and trotted several bodylengths away with her back to the embers. Shale left off his absent pacing when she approached. "How's your friend?"

"Sleeping. I tried not to hurt her earlier, but it was a hard chase. She'll need to go easy until she recovers."

"Mm." Shale digested this with a thoughtful nod. "Good to know we're on the right trail, though."

"One found, three to go." Kestrel frowned out into the darkness. "I saw the other two, at least, but there's still no sign of Mother."

He drew a cautious breath. "It's been a while, you know. How sure are you that she's there to be found?"

"Not at all." Her lips pulled back in the beginning of a snarl. "But that doesn't matter."

He sighed, face turned carefully away in the darkness. "I pity the bandit that'd try to take on my mother, but—I don't think I'd be looking for her as hard as you are for yours. Don't know if that's a good thing or not, but-" He shrugged. "That's what it is."

"You wouldn't?" Unplanned, her voice scaled upward in disbelief.

"I'd like to think I would. But she gave up so easily on Athren, it'd be pretty easy to give up on her."

She glanced at him inquiringly.

"They're well-off, my parents. We had all the best—food, trainers, horses. I still do, whether I want it or not, but when it was clear Athren would never have magic, our mother just...stopped. She didn't punish or disown him, she's not some wicked widow from a hearthtale, but she never put herself to any trouble for him again."

Kestrel snorted. "I'd toss her in the river. After Otter cleared it out." She thought. "Probably."

"Does Otter...?"

"No. He *can* change, there's just not much call for him to do it. But Mother never treated either of us as...as *less.*"

"Less? I'd have figured you for a model beastblood."

Her cheeks heated against the night air. "I'm good at what I do, but it was different when I was little." Shale's silence was somehow inviting, and she went on. "Hawk chicks are ugly, and I wasn't much different. I looked and acted strange enough that my birth mother couldn't bring herself to do more than feed me. At a distance. But Roe took me in, and she still tells embarassing baby stories about me and laughs. She never believed I was anything but delightful. I'm lucky to have her."

"Yeah?" Shale's glance took in her lean frame and travel-worn clothes, the boots that were as worn as the pads of her wolf-form. "I was thinking she was lucky to have you."

Chapter Eighteen

Whether from yesterday's exertions or her confused memories, Delver was still pale and quiet the next morning, and Kestrel paced several worried circles around their camp before she gave up and cornered Athren where he sat checking tack with his brother. "She's in no shape to move yet, and the others are getting further away by the hour. I don't know if they even *sleep*. I have to go find them."

"You do not." Deliberately, Shale set down the saddlebag he was cleaning. "They might be close enough for you to track alone—might—but do you want to risk whatever happened to that other beastblood? What's your brother going to do if you just start going west and forget to come back? If--"

She bared her teeth. "That's not fair. We always know there are risks, and right now my kin are walking right into them."

Shale sighed. "I'm not saying don't go, I'm saying don't go alone. If one of us rides with you, you can watch our backs and we'll watch yours, and the other one can stay back to look after the younger 'bloods."

Her skin prickled with the lift of nonexistent hackles. "I can't take much more looking, I want to *find* the problem. And hopefully bite it."

"Look, let me get Lace saddled and we'll head out together," Athren said. "I don't normally search while I'm riding because I can't pay attention to much else, but if you stay high enough to watch for trouble, I'll turn everything I've got to finding a—a trail for your people. And if Delver bolts again for some reason, Shale will know."

The stoneblood nodded. "I can stop her without hurting her. Maybe not a bird-shifter or a deer-shifter like you've described, but if she digs, I can keep her with us."

Reluctantly, she nodded. She tried to contain herself while Athren tended to his horse, but went back to prowling the edges of the camp until Otter harassed her into eating a bowlful of last night's leftovers. By the time she'd choked it down, Athren had his horse saddled; she snorted at Kestrel with what sounded like mild disgust, but didn't object to her nearness beyond that. Athren patted the mare's scarred shoulder and nodded at Kestrel.

"She's not carrying anything but me and a little emergency gear, so we can move fast. You said your two 'bloods weren't in a hurry, so we've got a good chance at catching up with them. I'll be focusing mostly on finding them, so just keep me from blundering into trouble, all right?"

"All right."

He jammed the oilcloth hat over his head to shield against the morning sun. Kestrel didn't see whatever signal he used to nudge the mare into motion, but she trotted off briskly toward the west. Kestrel followed them a moment later, taking to the sky on broad hawk's wings for endurance.

She coasted overhead at a comfortable distance through most of the morning, riding the occasional thermal upward for a better look at their surroundings. The wind-rippled grass hid wolves and coyotes, but neither in sufficient numbers to threaten a horse and rider even without Kestrel's presence. She could see the occasional flicker of ground birds or small game through the thinning cover, but they were moving normally and unaware of any danger. She could tell from Athren's loose posture that he was paying little or no attention to the land around him, but he and the mare still moved as smoothly together as any wolf pack or flock of birds. How hard was it, learning that sort of teamwork with a creature whose mind you couldn't touch?

From a wolf's-eye perspective—or even Athren's, riding shoulder-high through the plains grasses—the plains looked normal. But at Kestrel's height, the shallow dips and rise of earth beneath her were making her uneasy. The grass was...odd somehow. Some was drying normally with the onset of autumn, pale gold blades and swelling seedpods lightening the green waves beneath her; some was drying sword-stiff and brittle or turning to ashy grey, as if it had been dead for months rather than ripening with the turning of the year. The pale, scattered patches spotting the smooth sweep of plains beneath her made her think of a disease-mottled pelt or misborn pup, and her feathers slicked tight against her body for an unhappy moment. Remote as it was, the greenbloods should have been aware of this long ago.

Athren waved her down to talk just before the sun reached its peak. She glided down and dropped to the ground at a respectful distance from his mare. "What's wrong?"

"Not necessarily wrong. We're getting closer faster than I'd expected, but I think it's because your 'blood have stopped moving. Still alive," he added hastily as Kestrel's eyes began to widen. "Either they're resting or they've gotten where they were going."

She breathed out against a sudden surge of hope and fear. "Delver said she didn't stop unless she was too tired to ride at all. How far are they?"

"Three, maybe four hours at this pace." He shifted in the saddle. "I think I should probably hang back when we get close, let you get a look at the situation without being seen. Whatever you did to wake Delver up, I don't know if it'll work twice."

"Neither do I. Tine is three or four times my size if he shifts, and I can't think of a way to corner Finch without hurting him. But if I can see what's dragged them all this way, maybe I can find a way to counter it."

He nodded, but dubiously. Kestrel couldn't blame him. "Then let's see what we're dealing with."

Back in hawk-shape, she flapped to Athren's heavily-wrapped arm and let him launch her upward, sparing her a little of the laborious climb to scouting height. Otter often gave her the same sort of lift when they were looking for game, but this hunt mattered considerably more than a night's dinner.

She traced low, swift circles around Athren, kiting upward to look ahead only when the wind gave her an opportunity. She had just enough height to warn the Rider of dangers on his path, dropping down once to show him the way around a patch of shoulder-high grass with barbed blades and a dark rim of what looked like poison gleaming around their edges. Small rodents and dying plants littered the edges of the patch, the plants curved and knotted into forms that looked almost animal-like in their complexity. No time for a closer look, but she *had* to report it to the greenbloods when she could.

With Athren safely around the patch of poison, Kestrel soared back up for a clear look at the terrain. Pale cliffs rose at the edge of her vision in the northwest, the sheer stone unsoftened by greenery and looking strange after so many days of scrubby trees and tall grass. West of the trampled earth where she'd found Delver, a faint trail of bent grass marked what she assumed was Finch and Tine's trail; behind and below her, she saw Athren angle to cross it. Farther west, the grasses trembled with what she thought was a passing barkhide or other large beast, until her tentative mental query met only empty silence.

Blight.

With a quick glance down at Athren, she drove herself higher until she could see the disturbance more clearly: mounted men, moving steadily east and examining the trail beneath them.

Rot *and blight.*

She rose as far as the hawk's stocky, broadwinged shape could take her, keeping half an eye on Athren's distant form but focusing on the men below her. No hope of overhearing them at this height, but their behavior was easy enough to analyze even without speech. One tracker, peering at the trail and surrounding vegetation, and two guardians, riding with hands loose and ready and eyes scanning their surroundings. The horses had hardscrabble muscles but glossy coats, sleek with a layer of fat that only came from good feed and meticulous care. The body language and mismatched weaponry was all bandit, but they looked far too comfortable—too successful—to be out here so far from easy prey. Nothing out there for them to hunt except--

    She folded her wings, dropped a dozen manlengths in half as many heartbeats, and raced east to find Athren.

Chapter Nineteen

Kestrel came down low and fast by Athren's shoulder, backwinging to a stop just out of kicking range from his startled horse. "No farther. Trouble."

He blinked, shaking himself away from his search and reaching for his crossbow. "What kind? Where?"

She outlined what she'd seen as succinctly as possible, with her best impressions of speed and distance. "They're still out of scent range for the moment."

"So we can still avoid them, if we move before their horses get wind of mine and try to make friends." Athren scowled his way back to focus, his eyes sharpening with gratifying speed. "What did they act like?"

"Purposeful. Hunting..." She thought hard over what she'd seen. "No, tracking. Looking for something in particular, not just keeping an eye out. I thought maybe they were looking for us, but I don't see how they'd know about us."

"No reason they would." His lips thinned. "But they do know about Delver."

"You think they're tracking her?" She glanced back the way they'd come, eyes narrowing.

"I think it's likelier than looking for us. Think about it. All three of your people were heading west; you turned her off the trail, and the other two stopped sometime between last night and this morning. If they were expecting three beastblood and only two showed up..." He trailed off with an eloquent shrug.

Kestrel swallowed. "Then the first thing to do is to get Delver out of easy reach. Can you go back to camp and start everyone moving? I can probably confuse the trail and slow the trackers down by a bit, but I have to start now if it's going to be believable."

"Right. I'll backtrack us to the nearest stream; there's a gully there that'll keep us out of sight. These men sound pretty sharp; do you really think you'll be able to throw them off for long?"

Her laugh was half-choked by fear, but it was genuine nonetheless. "I've spent half my life in the mind of one hunter or another. I can do this."

She could. But it was harder than she expected.

Skimming just above the grass, she crossed the western trail again and backtracked until she found the place where she'd scuffled with Delver. Any decently competent tracker would be able to tell that something had happened here, so she set herself to leaving a new and clearer set of signs. A tuft of wolf-fur caught on a thorny vine, a clawed footprint where the grass grew thin...she passed the burrow where Delver had almost escaped and carefully tore the entrance apart.

She panicked and a wolf got her, nothing more to look for here. Really.

She'd seen no dogs or anything else to suggest the bandits could scent-track her, but she trotted north anyway, leaving a few more brindled hairs caught in the grass stems before she took to the air again. If she could circle back and intercept the bandits, she might be able to learn something, learn *anything* that might help her tease this mystery into some sort of order. She coasted over the waving grasses until she heard measured hoofbeats, then dropped down into cover and a stealthy feline shape. It felt strange, being in an environment so alien to the mountain cat's instincts, but it was far less likely she'd be spotted like this than as one of the enormous, sabertoothed plainscats.

Ears cupped to catch the slightest sound, she eased her way deeper into the grass. The vibration of hooves thrummed through her pads, and she crouched low to keep out of sight. She could just see the tips of the horses' ears as they neared her, the lead rider occasionally muttering to himself as he leaned down to examine the trail. Accustomed to doing her tracking by scent, Kestrel tried to guess what he was looking for, and her ears flicked anxiously backward as he reached the false trail she'd laid.

"Something happened here," he said to the other two bandits. "Blight if I know what, though. Looks like something lit after that last one, but there's no blood." He dismounted and bent down for a look at the claw furrows Kestrel had left in the earth.

"Animals wouldn't attack a beastblood, would they?" one of the escorts asked.

"One beastblood can't control 'em all, the boss says." The tracker ran an exploratory finger over the torn grass. "And if--"

The rising breeze ruffled Kestrel's fur, carrying her scent to the horses nearby. One bandit swore and grabbed for the tracker's shying mount, but the older one stayed firmly in the saddle, his eyes peering past his horse's pricked ears and one hand on his spear shaft. "Something in the grass. Mount up."

Hackles rising, Kestrel backed slowly away, paws feeling for any rustle or snapping twig that might betray her. The senior bandit rode a few cautious paces toward her, probing with his spear tip before he pivoted and swung it in a sweeping arc that left her utterly exposed.

She froze for an instant, then whirled and shot toward for the deep grasses. If she stayed on the ground, there was still a chance that they'd take her for a natural predator.

"That's a forest cat," the tracker said sharply. "Beastblood. Shoot it."

Blight! She flattened her ears as a bolt whizzed over her, its passage fanning the fur over her spine. She raced for the dubious shelter of the tall grass, one rider pounding in her wake and someone behind her shouting about disabling shots. A mountain cat couldn't outpace an unburdened horse for long, but she might be able to widen the lead between herself and the bandits. At least for long enough to get out of sight and change to something small that could go unseen. She knew the terrain better than her pursuers, and that might be enough to give her an edge.

Claws digging into the earth, she whipped her tail sideways to counterbalance and swerved sharply toward the eroded gully she'd overflown that morning. The next crossbow shot flew wide, but the one after that smacked the earth just shy of her hind feet; shooting to wound, not kill. After what she'd seen of Delver, that was less than reassuring. And she was tiring fast; cats were sprinters, not endurance runners. But the bandit chasing her was farther back now, and he didn't know the extent of her abilities.

Lungs burning, she pushed herself the final lengths to the gully she'd been seeking, and half-ran, half-tumbled over its edge. With the line of sight broken, she had a moment or two to act. She flattened herself against the eroded wall beneath a dangling fringe of grass and concentrated. Most shifting came as easily as breath for her, but the shape she needed was so often and so thoroughly corrupted that it was hard to construct a functioning body. But nothing could beat a barkhide for camouflage, if she could complete the shift in time.

Reptile at the base, weasel-quick in the summer and a lurking danger in the cold. A long, almost equine head on a sinuous neck, a lean, tough skeleton; most importantly, malleable scales with a rough, shimmering surface that took color and texture from their surroundings. The cat's laboring heart and sore pads slowly faded from her awareness, replaced by endless patience and a bone-deep awareness of the sun that no furred creature could match.

Kestrel closed her slitted eyes, curled her head and neck into an angular mass that looked like a pile of stones, and let her color shift to mirror the mottled amber and streaky green-gold of the ground around her. Her scales elongated into narrow, curved blades that blended with the tumbled pebbles and sparse grass, and she froze into motionlessness as the first bandit pulled up at the edge of the gully.

She had no external ears now, but she could feel the baffled, angry vibrations of their conversation all along her skin. The tracker's gaze swept over her twice, but she kept her eyes down and trusted to the mottled earth and her own camouflage to save her. If her heart was racing with human fear, the reptile's deadly stillness concealed it, and after a long, frustrated interval they turned away to search up and down the gully. The tracker headed back to the trail and the other two separated to ride the gully in different directions; they wouldn't be gone long, but it gave Kestrel a window of escape.

When she could no longer feel hoofbeats in her sensitive scales, Kestrel crept forward and pulled herself out of the gully with needle-sharp claws. It took her a moment to gather her strength for bird-form; only the thought of trying to find the others by scent alone gave her the strength to clamber into the air.

Chapter Twenty

Wings beating heavily for height, Kestrel climbed laboriously until she saw a line of trees following what looked like a shallow stream. Athren had planned to take the others and meet with her somewhere along the stream, so she angled her flight that way, coasting low and slow until she caught a glimpse of horsehide and metal through the trees. It was hard to see the camp from any significant height; there was no fire, and the bedrolls were hidden behind a screen of tangled vines. But Otter had been watching for her; she heard his sharp whistle a moment before she saw him scramble down from one of the trees.

She fluttered to a careful landing beneath the trees, dried leaves spinning away in the wind from her wings. The campsite was sheltered enough—and more importantly, hard to find—with a thin trickle of water nearby and low, dense trees screening them from easy view. Even in the afternoon light, the little copse was dimly lit and shaded. "What happened?" Otter demanded as she came out of bird-form with a weary shiver. "Athren said you were close behind him, and then you never showed up."

"Tracker. And bandits. And lots of running away." She flexed her sore hands. None of the crossbow bolts had hit her, but the frantic race had taken its toll on her regardless.

"They saw you?" Athren asked sharply. He'd come up behind Otter with a bridle looped over his arm, and now looked ready to turn around and put it back on his horse again.

"Bad luck. One of the horses winded me when I was trying to get a better look."

"You went back to spy on them? Blight it all, *check* with me—or whatever partner you've got—next time. We've been worried, your brother especially."

"Fisher, too." Otter scowled at her. "What were you *thinking*?"

She drew back a little. She was used to mutual glaring and growling with Otter, the verbal equivalent of pups tussling in the den, but earnest anger from her brother was startling. Her shoulders squared. "I was thinking that we need all the information we can get. We're all but blind here."

He uncrossed his arms, hands curving at his sides in a clawlike gesture she normally only saw on herself. "And we'll be worse off if you get shot! Or—or whatever happened to Delver and the rest. Which we still don't know."

"Which I was trying to find out-"

"*No,* Kess!" She could hear the snarl building in his voice. "We need you here and planning, not just bolting off on your own because you're the fastest."

"I *am* the fastest!" She wanted to snarl right back, but old fear and fresh frustration tangled in her throat and choked it off. "I'm the oldest left and the most experienced. If I'm not the first line of defense, who is?"

"The person we hired especially to help us? The one who can throw rocks with his mind? Me? *Blight*, Kestrel, I'm not that incompetent!"

"I didn't say that!"

"But you don't trust anybody else to do the important stuff. Or the dangerous stuff. Ever."

"I didn't think-"

"Then *start*!" He was almost nose to nose with her, pulse thumping visibly in his neck. "At least enough to work with the rest of us and not leave me wondering if you've been killed or taken."

Her instincts were clamoring too hard for the release of four feet and claws to speak. Spinning on her heel, she dropped into wolf-shape and stalked to the edge of camp, where she turned her back and pointed her nose out toward the plains. If no one trusted her scouting, she would blighted well keep watch instead.

The sun sank lower. In fox-shape, Fisher trotted up from behind her, examined her thoughtfully, and curled up against her ribs. After an interval of watching the blowing grass and listening to the rustle of birds and rodents, she heard casual footsteps behind her.

"We used to have a cat that sulked about like that," Shale said, dropping into a cross-legged seat a respectful distance away. "He'd come in all proud with a vole or scuttlefish, and then my mother would yell and shoo him off. And he'd sit with his back turned and glare at the wall until Athren or I tried to make him feel better."

Kestrel flicked an unimpressed ear at him.

"I promise I won't try to feed you a fish head, at least. Even if it did work on the cat." Shale sighed. "He was worried. We all were. Fisher was going around with the biggest eyes I've ever seen on anything short of an owlet. But I'd have done the same thing, for what it's worth. And probably have gotten yelled at just as hard."

She tilted her head inquiringly without quite condescending to look at him.

"I'm used to solving every problem I run across because there's nobody else who *can*. Figure it's probably the same way for a beastblood. But this is a human problem, not a magic one. Probably best to involve the rest of the humans before charging in."

She huffed and put her head down on her paws.

"Well. I probably wouldn't be impressed either."

He settled into a surprisingly comfortable silence, fingertips brushing over the ground in much the same absent way that Kestrel reached out to sense nearby predators. The quiet nagged at her until she finally snapped out of wolf-shape. "I want to know what's going *on*, blight it all!"

"So do I," Shale said quietly. "You're not the only one worrying—our mother is safely back in Threeshores, and I haven't heard of any normal people going missing in quite the same way as your kin. But Riders are...pretty much betwixt and between...whatever's happening, I'm as afraid for Athren as I am for me."

She knew *that* feeling down to her bones. But all she could say was, "Yeah."

On the way back into camp, she stopped to talk to Otter for a moment. "I'm not really sorry. But I don't think you're incompetent, and when this is over, you can yell at me all you want. All right?"

"Sort of."

Over a cold supper, Otter gradually lost his narrow eyes and hunched shoulders, but it was still a tense meal. As Fisher was gravely handing out wedges of travel bread, Kestrel threw up her hands in exasperation. "All right, we're not exactly working at cross-purposes, but none of us have enough information. There's something dangerous to the west, and I don't know how many of us are in danger. Time to put our goods on the scales and see what we've got."

"If we *had* goods," Otter muttered. "You're right, Kess, we don't know enough."

"We know those bandits were looking for Delver specifically. And they were able to recognize Kestrel as beastblood." Athren frowned. "That's what worries me; if they're not looking for beastblood to help them, what *are* they looking for?"

"There's been a few strange sightings to the south," Shale said. "Buildings with stoneblood power behind them but no—no skill. If someone were paying or even coercing one of us, the skill would still be there. Add in the bandits out there and I have to wonder if somebody's found a way to control 'blood power without going through the 'bloods themselves."

"I wasn't really thinking before you caught up with me," Delver said softly. "I could feel a little bit, I guess you'd say...it felt like somebody needed me." She frowned, distracted. "Not *me* me, just—like when you're tanning hides and you reach for a scraper. Any one'll do."

Shale grimaced. "Like the stoneblood I ran up against down south. Wouldn't be surprised if they'd acted just like Delver—no offense, Delver."

She shrugged. "It happened. Why get offended?"

Athren's eyes narrowed in thought, fingers drumming on his knee. "Kestrel was right. We do need more information. As remote as these plains are, somebody could build up a nice little warband before anyone noticed."

"But what would that have to do with missing 'bloods?" Kestrel asked. "Even if somebody can tap the magic, they can't use it for much without the skill."

"Crude control is still more than most people have," Shale said. "Shake the earth, kill plants or send them into overgrowth, chase the game away...that doesn't take subtlety, that's the kind of stuff we learn before we get the experience to do *real* work."

Otter shifted uneasily. "What worries me is if the rest of us are in the same danger. Delver doesn't remember what happened, and Fisher only remembers Roe talking to herself. We don't even know what signs to watch for."

Kestrel shook her head. "Whatever happened, it reached from here all the way to home. There's no safe place until we figure out what this is."

Chapter Twenty-One

Dinner was an uneasy affair, and by the time the stars were out, they were no closer to an answer.

"All right," Athren said finally, leaning back against one of the saddles he'd set up as backrests around the fire. "First step, I think, is a *planned* spying run."

"Still not sorry," Kestrel muttered.

"Still not expecting it," Otter retorted.

Athren rubbed the bridge of his nose. "Kestrel and I would probably be the best team, unless you think Delver or Otter could get closer?"

Kestrel took a breath to argue, then let it out and drummed her fingers on the ground instead.

"Doesn't matter," Delver said. "Closer I get, the likelier I am to wind up like before."

Otter frowned. "You think so?"

"It happened once. Still don't know *how*, much less how to stop it. You two haven't had anything like that happen."

"She's got a point," Shale said. "The rest of you—and me—haven't been affected yet. Could be because we're on our guard, could be just because they don't know we're out here-"

"Whoever 'they' are."

"That's what we're trying to learn." Athren visibly suppressed a sigh, but kept his hands at his side this time. "I have the training and Kestrel has the eyes for this. Unless there's any major objections?"

"As long as you don't get shot," Shale said.

Otter frowned but shrugged unhappily when Kestrel caught his eye; he knew as well as she did that his talents weren't much help in the midst of tall grass and shallow streams. "I'll try not to get shot either."

"You do that."

Athren glanced up at the stars. "Best to get moving, since one of us can see in the dark. Kestrel, I'll be able to get in a good deal closer than you think, so stick close by me, all right?"

Dubiously, she nodded. He was tall and rangy and there was little cover on the plains; where was he planning to hide?

Shale clapped his brother on the shoulder. "I'll keep the horses tacked until I hear from you. The rest of you, be ready to ride if something goes sour, but try to sleep otherwise."

Fisher crossed her arms and scowled, and Otter grumbled deep in his throat. "Easy for you to say."

"It is. That's why I'm staying up on watch; I can worry better that way."

Athren rummaged through his packs, came out with a mottled cloak and leather tube, and started saddling his horse. The mare snorted unhappily and cocked a hind hoof in the same mock-threatening way that Kestrel sparred with Otter, but she tolerated the bridle with reasonably good grace. "Horses have decent night-sight," he informed her over his shoulder. "Better than mine. And she's trained to put up with any number of strange requests from me, so following an—owl? Is that what you're going to do?--should be easy enough."

"Owl to start, yes. Cat by preference if I need to touch down, maybe a fox if I need to hide. Here, let me show you some of how beastblood talk when they're shifted..."

They left camp at a brisk walk while Kestrel explained the most basic and most important signals she used to communicate with other 'blood. *Run, hide, freeze, fight* and *trouble* figured prominently, and she bit her lip as she stared worriedly westward.

"I can't tell you it'll be all right," Athren said. "I keep thinking I should, it's what I'd say to any other client. But I can tell you that the Riders train for scouting missions like this, and I think between the two of us, we can learn what we need to and get back to the others safely."

"And if we can't?"

"Then we can't." He tugged a polished stone oval on a leather string out from under his shirt, showed it to her, and tucked it back out of sight. "Shale will know if I'm badly hurt or dead. If it goes bad, he'll get the rest to safety one way or the other. And if I can get on Lace, I can get away from pretty much anything. So look out for yourself and we'll see what we can do."

Provisionally reassured, she lifted into the night sky on soft-feathered wings. She couldn't reach the heights in owl-form that she could as a hawk, but sight and sound were clear enough to lead her unerringly to the bandits' trail. She swooped down to attract Athren's attention, then led him on a parallel path to give him a running start if the trail was guarded.

She glided noiselessly above the trail, her owl's vision picking out every detail down to broken stems and shed horse hairs. Below her, Athren rode at a tight, wary trot, shoulders tense and head turning continually with none of the loose-limbed ease he'd shown earlier. With the wind lifting her, she was able to swing away from the trail in long, shallow arcs, and at the farthest point of one she saw a distant curl of white smoke against the starry sky. She took a moment to memorize its position against the stars, then dipped down to meet Athren.

"Smoke. West-northwest." She could just smell it in human form, grassy-sweet dried dung with an unpleasant latrine undertone.

"Do you think that's our bandits?"

"Probably." She took a slow breath, searching the predators nearby. "I can smell the smoke from here, and nothing nearby is scared of any sort of wildfire."

"All right. Lead the way."

She eased into the mountain cat's shape, eyes wide to catch every mote of light, and prowled into the tall grass.

"Slow *down*," Athren said after a moment. "Or I'll tie a ribbon on your tail."

She tilted her head in a gesture of apology he was unlikely to understand, and turned her ears back so he could see their white markings in the darkness. The cat's senses read the smoke-scent better than her human nose could, sorting through the campfire smell to find hints of metal, human bodies, horses, and...dogs, maybe? Something canine, with no trace of fox-musk. It was a rarity; there were nomadic hunters to the northeast who traveled with dogs, but for most people a domesticated meat-eater was far too dangerous a liability.

She saw the change in Athren's posture when he caught the scent that she'd been following, and stopped worrying about guiding him accurately. Instead, she circled to keep them upwind of the camp. She might be able to silence dogs, but an experienced tracker would probably be watching for horses to alert as well. Just out of canine scent-range, she left the cat-shape behind and stood to put a hand on Athren's bridle.

"Any closer and they'll be able to scent us," she murmured. "Stay where I can see you and I'll do the same, all right?"

Athren nodded briskly and unrolled his cloak, a long, raggedy thing with pale, irregular patches like a resting barkhide's scales. "It's not perfect camouflage, but it'll help. Especially in the dark." He slid out of the saddle with an affectionate pat to Lace's shoulder, and pulled the reins over her head to brush the ground. "She'll wait unless I call her. Let's go."

Kestrel melted into the grass with Athren close behind her, straining her ears for any hint of danger. No sound from the camp but a distant buzz of conversation, nothing new on the wind but a touch of distant deer-scent. As they approached the rise just ahead of the bandit camp, canine presences flickered dimly in her mind, and she slowed to reach out for them. Her connection with dogs was fitful at best, but if she could see through their eyes...

For a heartbeat, she reached a tentative rapport with one, then the pack—then she snapped loose with a muted snarl of shock and outrage, tail switching in a long whiplash arc.

"Kestrel?"

The snarl built to a bone-deep growl, rumbling from throat to belly to claws. Someone *dared?*

"Kess." Athren's palm landed tentatively between her shoulders, then lowered with a little more confidence. "Talk to me."

With difficulty, she left the cat-shape behind, the snarl translating to a hissing indrawn breath as she struggled for control. "I am going to rip someone's spine out. Frontways."

"Not volunteering. What happened?"

She let out a short, harsh breath. "I thought they were using dogs. Trained dogs. But those are wolves. Those are *mine.*"

"Wolves? There's a beastblood controlling them?"

"No, there's some magicless—*misborn*—controlling them. Somehow. He won't let them think, won't let them *move* unless he's paying attention." Her fingers flexed, released, and flexed again, nails beginning to hook and thicken.

"He?"

"When the wolves feel him, I can too. Shale's right; there's power there, but no skill."

"Anything else you can tell?"

"I can tell he's going to die. They're not *tools*."

"Besides that."

"Not yet."

"Right. No killing anybody until we learn everything we can, all right?" Athren dropped to the ground and crawled on knees and elbows to the top of the rise, where he pulled a package from his pocket and unwrapped two transparent discs. The curved surfaces gleamed in the moonlight as he fitted the leather tube around them with absent ease and lifted it to his face. "Not as good as a hawk's eyes, but better than most," he murmured when Kestrel peered at him curiously. "Give me a few more heartbeats...there."

His lips thinned in concentration. Kestrel waited.

"All right, I see your wolves. Four bandits moving, four small tents, figure two to a tent plus whoever's in that big one in the middle. Wolves are...you're right, that's unpleasant to watch. Sitting and staring straight ahead, plus a couple of those big cats with the teeth doing the same thing. Can't see 'em, but I can feel two, maybe three beastblood, think they're in that oversized tent."

Kestrel nodded on a sharp intake of breath. Reluctantly, she said, "If they've been in a state like Delver all this while, another night probably won't change things. Let me circle around and find another place for you to spy from."

Spyglass still raised, he nodded, and she took off as an owl once more. A quarter-circle of the camp, and she found a concealed vantage point that gave him a good view of its layout. Tentatively, she reached out to the disoriented wolves, tamping down rage and revulsion to watch through their eyes. The bandits were well-organized but clearly moving of their own volition, with two standing watch, one cooking, and three tending to the same mundane camp chores that Kestrel had gotten used to. As one of them checked the porridge over the central fire, the wolves stood in unison, and Kestrel jerked her awareness away at the secondhand touch of an unfamiliar mind.

She circled above the firelight's reach, listening to snippets of conversation as the tracker she'd already encountered ladled out bowls of food. Mice rustled in the grass and somewhere a deer's hooves drummed the ground, but none of the wolves so much as twitched an ear or moved when a portion of food landed on the dirt before them. Her talons clenched with the desire to break them free of that unnatural control.

The doorflap of the biggest tent twitched open, and Finch and Tine walked out to the campfire. She almost dove for them, but brought her traitorous wings under control with an effort. Their faces were unnervingly placid, the faint tug of their presence muted almost to nonexistence, and as they accepted their bowls of porridge, they dropped to sit crosslegged and began to eat in perfect synchrony. At the same time, the wolves dipped their heads and began to eat, jaws moving in rhythm with one another. Kestrel's feathers slicked back against her body, the night going briefly darker as her pupils contracted in fear. Whoever was behind this might have usurped a beastblood's connection, but this kind of rigid control was nothing a beastblood *could* do.

Shivering, she glided back down to Athren. "See them?" he asked on a barely audible breath.

She inclined her head.

"Haven't seen a leader, but we've got a good idea of layout and numbers now. Best to get out before our luck changes. Something's got every animal *except* your wolves riled up. Ready?"

Kestrel ruffled her feathers. *Ready.* More than ready. If she couldn't kill the one who was using her wolves, she wanted away from here until she could.

She folded her wings and dropped into cat-shape, crouching low in the grass as she backed away from their vantage point. Her head snapped up at a sudden whiff of deer, *close* deer, and why in all the world would a deer approach a cat and a human from downwind? Hunter's instincts sharpened her perceptions before she wondered what a white-tail doe was doing this far from the sheltering trees, and before the doe's muzzle dipped to brush the top of her head. The scent was...was blurred by travel, by dust and rain and surviving on grass alone. But the eyes, the stance, the *presence* were all familiar, and Kestrel lost the cat-shape in her shock.

"--mother?"

Chapter Twenty-Two

"Well, get her *out* of there, then!" Athren looked from Kestrel to the doe and back. "Somehow."

"This isn't like Delver. She knows me." She turned back to Roe. "Otter's safe. So is Fi—um, the fox kit."

Roe's taut posture softened, and she let out a relieved breath. Kestrel rested her forehead against her mother's for a moment, before the doe nudged her in the ribs and flicked her nose imperiously eastward.

"Right. Back to camp, and we'll talk." She frowned. "*Can you change?*"

Roe tilted her head noncommittally; too complicated for a yes-or-no answer.

"Then let's go."

In wolf-shape for distance running, she paced anxious circles around the other two as they made their way back to Athren's horse, her ears swiveling to catch any sound from the bandits behind them. The wolves in camp were aware of her presence but didn't react to it; whatever control their enemy had over them, he didn't or couldn't get information from them.

Once they were out of earshot and Athren safely mounted, she switched to a swift, steady pace, staying a whisker behind the deer and mare to keep an ear out for trouble from behind. But the distance passed by easily, and Kestrel fell into a comfortable lope at Roe's shoulder, remembering long-ago games of tag where Roe had helped her learn how to control her growing power and ungainly cub's body. Hide-and-seek for the mind, tag for the body, laughter and easy conversation when it was all done. The memories were warm as sunlight, and she matched her pace to the beat of hooves beside her. For a few minutes, her fears were swallowed up in wolf-instincts and the ease of companionship.

Shale met them a stone's throw away from camp, his face drawn into sleepless lines that eased a little when he saw the three of them. "Kestrel's mother? Pleased to meet you."

Kestrel gave him a weary smile and looked around until she found a lump of blankets that looked like Otter, then gave a low whistle to wake him. He scrambled to his feet, shoving the blankets behind him, but his nose alerted him to Roe's presence before his bleary eyes. "You *found* her?"

"She found us."

Roe closed her eyes, flattened her ears in concentration, and shifted away from the deer-shape after an unnervingly long interval. She was travel-worn and underfed, but her eyes were still alert and she looked at both her children with clear recognition. Everything Kestrel had wanted to say tangled together, and she flung her arms around her mother a moment before Otter hit them both like an avalanche.

"So good to see you again," Roe murmured into both their hair.

A flicker of motion caught Kestrel's eye, and she moved to make room for a hesitant Fisher. Roe looked over her shoulder to the fox-sized tangle of blankets next to Otter's bedroll.

"Looks like you're one of ours now," she said to the little girl. "Come here."

Fisher didn't argue.

Roe shepherded them over to Otter's blankets in preference to the chilly ground, and sat down unceremoniously with Fisher in her lap and Otter and Kestrel on each side. "I know you have questions—*I* have questions," she added with a sharp glance at all three of them. "But I don't have long to stay human-"

"Why not?" Otter demanded.

"I mentioned questions, didn't I? The important thing is, you're in danger."

Kestrel nodded. "We know that. Know how to shake it off, a little. But we don't really know what or why. What *happened* to you? To all of you?"

Roe swallowed, staring out into the darkness. "Someone out there can control 'bloods. Any sort, I think, but he got to us easily enough. I was...I *think* I was in the stillroom with the little one-"

"Fisher," the girl said in a small voice.

"With Fisher, and suddenly it seemed like the most obvious thing to do was to mount up and ride west. Like I'd been planning to do it for days. If I hadn't been wondering how to take a fox cub along, I'd have left with Crane and the cousins right then. As it was, I wondered how and then I wondered *why,* and that bought me a little breathing room."

"But you didn't try to get away?"

"I couldn't think that well, just enough to realize someone was trying to control me the way I would a stampede or something. Crude, but strong. I wanted to get out of reach before it found Fisher, too. So I hid her, told her to wait for you, and-" She made an eloquent gesture at her bedraggled state. "I ran."

Otter's shoulders pulled in on themselves. "But why just— out? You knew the route we were on, why not look for us?"

"Otter...I didn't know much of anything by then. Whoever, whatever it is, it was looking for a human mind and the only way I could keep it out was to be as *un*-human as I possibly could. I knew...priorities, people, but not really names or places. I remembered that the cousins were in danger, so I tried to follow them without being seen, until I scented you and it made things come clearer. I don't think I could have changed back without you or Kestrel here with me."

He huffed in reluctant laughter. "We found Delver and pretty much scared her back to her senses. Don't think Kess would've had the nerve to try that on you."

"Nope," Kestrel admitted without a trace of embarrassment.

Roe sagged against the two of them. "Then maybe there's a chance to bring the others back."

"And keep it from happening again." If anybody thought she was going to go back on patrol and wait for disaster like this to strike again...

Roe leaned her head against Kestrel's for a moment. "Maybe. I'll be just as happy to stay safely hidden, if we can manage *that*."

Kestrel woke in bear-form, curled protectively as far around the other three as she could manage. Roe slept with her hooves tucked under her and Fisher leaning against her side, soaking up the warmth in boneless contentment, but Otter woke up surly as soon as Kestrel moved.

"Don't *do* that," he grumbled, scrubbing at his itching nose. "Was dreaming about waterweed in my nose half the night with all that fur."

"I didn't do it on purpose, I was worried."

As Fisher carefully mixed the remains of last night's food into a tolerable porridge, Kestrel cast her awareness as widely as possible. She could feel a few hawks climbing the rising thermals, a low background thrum of foxes and ferrets, the far-off, thoughtful rumble of one of the sabertoothed plainscats...and a dull throb like a bruise from the controlled wolves at the very edge of her range. She breathed out and concentrated, vaguely feeling a supportive hand at her elbow as she focused on the distant wolves.

Whatever controlled them kept them dormant but paid them no more attention than necessary, and she risked a moment of deeper rapport to see what they saw. A billow of canvas, the snap of leather straps on tack and bedding, a glimpse of Finch and Tine sitting stock-still on bridleless horses, and a man in lightweight leather armor who turned his head curiously toward the wolves-

She severed the connection before he could meet her gaze through the wolf's eyes. "They're moving out. We need to catch up."

Shale released her arm as she blinked back to focus on her surroundings. "What did you see?"

"Packing up camp. I don't know where they're headed yet, but I may be able to look through the wolves without alerting that— that-"

"Sorcerer," Shale suggested. "Old word for a magic-user who's not necessarily 'blood."

"'Enemy' works better for me, but I still saw him. He's apparently given up on finding Delver and is moving on to— whatever's next."

"Which can't be good for Finch and Tine," Otter said.

Roe's ears tilted back in dismay.

Kestrel let out a short, worried breath, fingers curling against her palms. "No more scouting. We don't have enough information, but we don't have any *time* at all."

"You're right." Athren pulled out his miniaturized map. "I don't know what we're dealing with, but I can't see it going anywhere good. Or even harmless."

"So we find a way to keep Fisher and Delver safe-" Otter began. Delver took a thoughtful breath; Fisher just folded her arms and scowled.

"No. We eat and we *plan* and we do not go into this blind." Athren glared at all of them impartially.

"All right." Kestrel tugged Otter after her and gestured Athren and his brother closer to the fire. "Let's plan, then."

Chapter Twenty-Three

Kestrel wove tight, anxious circles high above the bandits' camp, wispy clouds shredding over her wingtips. Below her, three men were stowing the last of their tents and rolling them into a loose pile, while a fourth was saddling horses. Two more were dismantling the central tent, and one bandit stood careful watch on the low bluff above the camp, his posture alert but unconcerned. She could feel a faint whisper of beastblood presence, but it was distant and muted, just like the wolves lying in a neat double row at the edge of camp.

Her feathers pulled tighter against her body than the cool air could explain. Athren was trained for skirmishes, Shale had powers the bandits weren't anticipating, but it was her family and her charges down there, and the thought of failing either of them had haunted her all morning.

She was well out of easy sight distance, as high as an eagle could fly, and watching sharply for the signal to move. She could see Shale approaching the bluff with Roe at a cautious distance behind and kept a cautious eye on them; she might be watching Shale for his signal, but the rest were watching her.

A new figure stepped out of the central tent, and she tightened her circle to take in every detail. Well-fed and strangely unscarred, the bandit leader was splitting his attention between the two beastblood and the quiescent wolves, and Kestrel marked him in her memory. She'd had to kill humans a few times in her life, but this time she suspected it would be a relief.

A flicker of equine ears above the tall grass told her Athren and Otter were circling the camp, and icy air spiked through her as her breath quickened. One last check; the wolves' heads were all turned docilely toward the sorcerer, two plainscats looming behind them like spears in a quiver of crossbow bolts. If their plans played out correctly, they'd be able to rescue the two beastblood and get away cleanly. If not...they'd salvage what they could and she'd tear apart anyone trying to recapture her mother or Delver.

She saw a pale glimmer far below as Shale looked up in search of her, then dropped his hand by his horse's neck where it wouldn't alert the sentry. No more watching; time to hunt.

Kestrel folded her wings and dove. Below her, Shale slid from the saddle and rested his fingertips on the ground; the earth below the bandit sentry lost all cohesion and the sentry dropped straight down, a layer of glossy-smooth stone beginning to form where he'd stood. A flicker of russet fur and deliberate flash of a jackrabbit's white tail showed her where Delver and Fisher were headed for the horses, but she could spare no more time to look.

Be safe, *little sister!*

She drove straight for the wolves, feeling for their minds and shutting out all other concerns. There was a startled shout, then a hasty call to order as the first horse squealed and bolted, but most of her attention was elsewhere. She plunged down in front of the wolves with a flurry of wingbeats and a whiplash release of power, all her throttled outrage crackling along her nerves and into the captive animals. Steal her charges, steal her *kin*, and try to escape unmarked into the wilds?

The wolves' dazed acceptance shivered away under her contact like ice beneath a heavy footstep. No pack this, just a collection of whatever large animals their enemy had run across, but she could create that bond for a little while, share her mind and her goals with the wolves. She'd debate whether she *should* later, after her family was safe.

The two cats were too independent for her to pull into the temporary bond; the larger one spun and bolted for the plains and the smaller crouched defensively, looking around with a snarl. Kestrel leaped and changed to wolf-shape in midair, coming down in the middle of her temporary pack. Hidden in a cloud of milling wolves, she reached for the strongest mind among them, intending to rush the bandits. Then powerful feline thoughts shoved into her mind.

Trapped like mud, like vines. Couldn't hunt. Cubs cried, cubs starved. It wasn't grief as a human would know it, but it burned through the female plainscat, a constant helpless anger underlaid with the memory of fading kitten whimpers. *Hunt with you.*

Bristling with the cat's rage as well as her own, she pulled the cat into the pack and let it sweep her along, racing in an arc across the far edge of camp to drive the bandits into the center. Razor-edged shards of stone flew over their heads—calculatedly over their heads, Kestrel realized, and warned the pack to stay low.

With her awareness stretched across the pack, she heard Fisher's cheerful yap through ears that weren't her own. The fox cub wove nimbly through charging paws and hooves to drive the bandits' horses away, until a shrill whistle from Shale called her up to the bluff and relative safety. Across the camp, Athren's mare pivoted on her hindquarters and let him and Otter slide to the ground. Both of them dove for safety behind a pile of packed tents; Kestrel heard their crossbows cock and dashed away with the wolves to buy them time.

They'd had the upper hand for a moment, but even faced with sudden chaos and an angry wolf pack, the bandits were experienced fighters. They were rallying, and Kestrel yelped as a crossbow bolt took one of her wolves in the ribs. Two of them were taking shelter behind a downed horse, one man with a shield and sword was watching their backs, and there was a bowman climbing the bluff to get a clear field of fire-

She couldn't let him get up there, not with Shale unprotected and Fisher nearby. She left the wolves behind and flung herself upward, clawing for height in the dusty air. She caught Otter's startled glance as she struggled higher and dove, flying for the bowman's face with no concern for silence or subtlety. Otter and the rest were safe for the moment; what she needed now was *delay.*

Shrieking, Kestrel raked her talons across the bandit's face and scalp. Still kneeling on the bluff, Shale straightened with a jerk

and stumbled backward, reaching for the pouch of stones at his waist.

"Kess! Down!"

She dropped and hit the ground on four paws as jagged pebbles shot over her head and into the bandit's face and hands. She lunged as the bowman collapsed, setting teeth in his throat and ripping with a twist of her head. Her hackles lifted with distant unease, but she forced it aside; misgivings later, rescue now.

She wobbled for a disoriented moment; shifting itself took little effort, but the frequent changes to mindset and instinct were wearing her down. But she skidded down the bluff anyway, scanning the campsite as she dropped. Three bandits down or dead, two entirely too active, no sign of the sorcerer or the two beastblood. To her right, Otter was curled protectively around a bleeding arm and *blight* it why hadn't she watched him better?

She spun on her forepaws, sprinting past her brother and Athren toward the crossbowman who'd taken shelter behind a grounded horse. A tendril of thought reached out to the plainscat, who responded with a distracted *prey here not helping.* Kestrel snarled at the images that accompanied the brief communication; the bandit leader without a hair out of place, focused on Finch and Tine as they methodically tacked up three horses. Whatever he was doing with the cousins, he'd already abandoned his men.

A sharp, imperative bark for Otter and a jerk of her head toward where the plainscat had disappeared were all she had time for. A pause to reorient herself and gather her power, and she blurred into bear-form and charged, swatting the swordsman aside as she vaulted the dying horse. Thick hide and thicker fur absorbed most of the blow from the blade he swung at her, but she still roared at the gash across her ribs and hindquarters.

Behind her, Otter shouted and started to scramble over the piled tents; Athren yanked him back and sighted along his crossbow, looking for a clear shot. But there was no more time to spare for lesser prey when the vital target was so close; she spun and slapped at both bandits with a widespread paw, not caring if she killed or injured so long as she *moved.*

Kestrel pushed herself into an all-out gallop. Ashes from the campfire billowed up around her paws as she charged through the ember's, following the pull of the plainscat in her mind until she found a man who smelled of old stone and strange herbs. He stood with a hand rigidly outthrust toward the cat, clenched fist trembling as she snarled and swiped. But he'd regained enough control that the plainscat couldn't come closer to him.

"...mine, lie down," he muttered.

You can go free when he dies. She shared what strength she could with the cat, trading bear's shape for wolf's one more time. The ground felt cold and rough under her paws as she fought for focus, but after a dizzy moment she managed a carrying howl. Otter and Delver, at least, would recognize the call for what it was.

She dashed at the sorcerer to slash at his hands and disrupt his focus on the cat, then circled around to lunge for the great vein in his leg. The cat crouched and swiped with a foreleg, knocking him off his feet.

Dimly, she heard running feet in a familiar rhythm: Shale and Otter, with others just behind them. The cat's snarl built to a scream as the sorcerer's focus weakened and Kestrel leaped, jaws snapping haphazardly at his face and throat. Her fangs laid open the arm he threw up to shield himself, and the cat yowled with Kestrel's glee as she drew blood. In the camp beyond, the wolves broke off their own hunt to converge on her prey.

"I've got him. Back off, Kess, I don't know what touching him will do." Otter's sides were heaving, but he held the crossbow braced in a steady grip.

She growled. *He took my pack.* The images blurred together—family, friends, cubs, the wolves she'd fought with—and she couldn't quite remember which ones she meant.

"*Move,* Kess, I've got him!"

She'd expected curses, magic, or a war-cry. She hadn't expected the sorcerer to look at the gathering predators, the armed men, and the fangs at his throat, and *shrug.*

He whipped his head sideways for a pinpoint stare at Finch and Tine. "*West,*" he told them, shuddered, and went limp. For a heartbeat, the calculation in his eyes gave way to shock and outrage, and he began to struggle. Kestrel snapped, and the plainscat lunged past her and sank her saber teeth into his shoulder. Kestrel tumbled aside as the cat shook him like a fox with a snake, Otter winced at the sound of breaking bones, and Tine shifted shape into a tawny-furred elk and sprinted away from them. Finch fluttered overhead, both of them striking unerringly westward.

"Shale!" she cried, scrambling to her feet while the world tilted under her.

He reached for his pouch again, pulling out a weighted net and flinging it into the air after Finch. The bird-shifter dodged and the pebbles strung around the net swerved to follow him, wrapping around his wildly beating wings and returning to Shale in a long, sweeping arc. A frantic hand gesture, and the soil pulled itself into a wall in front of Tine, but the stag leaped over it and kept going.

Maybe I can at least track him. Kestrel tried to concentrate enough for one more shift, but Roe walked past her and planted her feet on the ground.

"Stop that." She stamped her foot, and the subtle hum of her mother's presence grew into a pulse of power that shook her bones. Tine stopped in his tracks. "Where do you think you're going?" Roe asked. Otter stifled slightly dumbstruck laughter in his hand. "Listen to *me,* not him. It's time to go home."

Shoulders square, she faced the young stag and held him with her gaze until the brink-of-flight tension eased out of his muscles.

"How is she-" Athren whispered.

"Experience? Same forms? She's drowning out the other one somehow."

Tine turned slowly and took a hesitant step back. Roe relaxed and shifted her stance to a more welcoming angle. "There we go. Let's get you home."

The stag stepped carefully closer, and finally dropped his muzzle to rest a fingerbreadth away from Roe's chin. She turned to stand at his shoulder, her relief all but palpable to the rest of the group. "He's not healed, but now he's listening to me and not that kinless bandit. Once we're safely home, I think we'll be able to get him back to normal."

Kestrel looked at the dead sorcerer and his expression of betrayal. She steeled herself. "I don't think we *can* go home. Not all of us, not yet."

"We can't," Otter asked, so flatly it sounded like a command.

"Whatever we were fighting...wasn't him." She grimaced. "I was right in his face when he died, and something *left* him, I saw it. I don't think he started this trouble, and he may have been controlled just as much as the wolves were."

Otter looked dubious and Shale concerned; Athren seemed to have so many arguments piling up that he couldn't pick the first one. "So if you're right, what on all the stones do you want to do about it?"

"Clean up what we can. Get the wounded—physically and mentally—an escort to safety. After that-" She let out a breath that turned into a half-hysterical giggle. "We find out what's in the west."

Chapter Twenty-Four

"Cleaning up" was more involved than Kestrel had suspected. They salvaged the bandits' travel rations, burned the bodies, and left their traveling gear where it was after Athren examined it and shoved it away with a dismissive snort. The plainscat snarled and swiped when any of them, even Kestrel, so much as looked at the sorcerer's body; tasting the roil of rage and bloodlust in those feline thoughts, Kestrel asked no questions when both cat and body disappeared.

She spent a worried half-hour considering the freed wolves before she huffed in exasperation, called them all back to her, and began painstakingly rebuilding the temporary pack-bond she'd constructed. Careful pressure dulled the melancholy of missing mates and siblings, and an even more gentle adjustment to their humours strengthened feelings of tolerance and tentative affection. It was delicate work, and when she released her contact with the last wolf, she leaned back and stretched with a sigh of relief.

"Thought you were just going to send them all away." Smelling of smoke and sweat, Shale came up by her shoulder. The tight skin around his eyes suggested as much stress as a lashing tail or raised hackles on another creature, but his posture was too tired for serious conversation.

"I planned to. But their first instinct would be to go looking for the rest of their pack, and most of these are too far from home to survive the search. So-" She waved a hand at the resting wolves. "New pack. It's not the best solution, but it's the one I've got."

His answering chuckle carried a wealth of fellow-feeling, but he didn't volunteer anything further, and they sat half-dozing in the lowering sun.

No one wanted to stay in the bandits' camp, so they set up their bedrolls in a wide, shallow depression a few miles to the west.

Kestrel volunteered for her habitual second watch until Roe glared her into submission.

"I may be half-fed and tired, but my ears are just as good as your eyes, child, and *I* wasn't wrestling bandits and running around with wolves all day. Sleep."

She slept. But not without throwing a handful of grass at the snickering Otter.

The next morning they took a cautious ride westward, with the less-susceptible Athren in the lead and the rest following in a scattered, single-file column. Roe rode just in front of Shale's rear position, with Tine in stag-form walking meekly beside her; sunk deep in cervine instincts and habits, he'd decided Kestrel's mother was the lead doe and was following her movements. Finch slept in bird-form in a box that Athren had cobbled together; they couldn't risk letting him free until they knew if the sorcerer's last command still drove him.

Kestrel took gingerly to the air to scout; the shallow slash she'd taken pulled and twinged with every wingbeat, but once she found a thermal to ride, she could stay still and just watch. The sun felt good on her wings, and the sight of all her kin trailing below like beads on a string eased the tension that had been driving her every hour, in every shape.

Gliding high above the tall grasses, she was the first to see the cliff that blocked the westward path. *All* the westward path, stretching off sheer and water-smooth as far on either side as her keen eyes could see. Topped with greenery that was impossibly lush in the late-summer sun, it rose sharp and straight from the plains, an abrupt expanse of sandy-gold stone that no natural process could have formed.

If she were less weary, she would have flown ahead and investigated. But instead she circled down to land on Otter's saddlehorn—his horse, long accustomed to flapping wings at this point, barely turned an ear in her direction—and signaled *obstacle, catch up.*

"Dangerous?"

Not yet.

He nodded and turned in the saddle to call back to Shale before urging his gelding into a trot. Too weary to climb another thermal, Kestrel dropped to the ground and loped ahead as a wolf.

She caught up to Athren near the base of the cliff; he and Delver had reined their horses to a halt at a safe distance and were watching for the rest. "This," he announced, "was not what I expected."

The cliff rose starkly out of the ground, its sandy sheen blending with the summer-dried grass around them. But the size, easily a dozen manheights or more, and glassy smooth surface were nothing natural, and the hair on the back of her neck lifted every time she looked at it. From the ground, the edge of the cliff looked utterly seamless, the simple line broken here and there by a plume of trailing vines from above. Kestrel narrowed her eyes. "That's nothing natural. Or human."

"What do you mean?"

She frowned, trying to trace the instinctive reaction back to something concrete. "Real cliffs erode, they have ledges, they have vines and birds that lodge themselves in little crannies. This looks like—like pottery. Or like Threeshores, if they hadn't built it for people to live in."

"You think this is stoneblood work?"

"Maybe? How *many* stoneblood?" Kestrel looked from one side to the other of the featureless wall.

"Think it's safe to touch?"

"One way to find out." She began to push through the waist-high grass in front of her.

"Kess!"

"Just grab me if I collapse or something."

"Or *wait* for the *stoneblood.*" Athren nudged his mare to block Kestrel's path, giving her a glare that could have rivaled one of Otter's.

"...or we could wait for Shale." Arms crossed, she sank to a seat on the ground.

But she was tired enough to just sit and feel the gentle push of sunlight on her skin, the silence was oddly comfortable, and Athren had lost the glare by the time Roe and Tine arrived, with Shale just behind them. Roe kept one wary eye on Tine, but the younger beastblood showed no inclination to investigate the cliff or to come out of deer-form. Roe looked searchingly at him, but shook her head after a moment.

"He doesn't recognize it. He remembers the command to go west, but nothing that was supposed to happen after that. I—well, more or less put him to sleep when we freed him, and he'll stay that way until we get to safety. I don't think he'll run, but by the same token, he can't tell us what he was running to."

"I don't think he knows," Delver said. "I didn't. Just direction, no plans."

"Then we'll have to find out on our own," Otter said.

Roe drew an indignant breath. "We're *safe*. We need to get to a decent distance before he, or they, or it finds us again."

"He found you all the way at home. How much further could we go?" Kestrel scuffed unhappily at the ground; it hurt to argue with her mother, but whatever was behind that cliff, she could feel it the same way a rabbit felt the fox's stare.

"We know how to avoid the control now."

"For a little bit. Maybe And I like flying, but I don't want to spend the rest of my life as a hawk. Mother, I know predators, and I *know* something up there wants us. If it's hungry, it's not going to stop just because it missed the first pounce."

Roe's sigh had a harsh edge to it, like a stag spoiling for a fight. Tine lifted his head to regard her in mild alarm. "Stones swallow it, I can't come *with* you, and I've left you unprotected all this time. I want to come back when we're well-rested and well-armed-"

"And with a pack of Threeshores' best militia," Delver muttered.

"-but you're right, if something's hunting 'blood, it may be too strong to fight by the time we can do all that."

"I can't swear one way or another, but something up there feels—if I found a bear or a panther that struck me like that, I'd kill it before it went rabid or turned man-eater. I'm sorry, I really am, I wish we could go home instead."

"So do I." Roe closed her eyes. "But you've come this far without me. Just—if it comes to running or dying, *run*."

"I'll make sure she does," Otter promised. With an effort, Kestrel tamped down her reflexive just-try-it sneer.

Roe turned away, shoulders set and eyes closed. "Best I can hope for," she said reluctantly after a moment. She looked up at the looming cliff. "But you'll never be able to get the horses up there. I can take them and the cousins to Valerian's steading to keep them safe until you're done here."

Shale looked over her thin and travel-worn state with concern. "We've got our horses and the bandits' as well. Will you be all right with all of those?"

"I'm *beastblood*. The day I can't handle a herd of horses—trained horses, at that—I'll move in with Valerian and start growing beets."

Athren nodded in provisional acceptance. "Then we'll divide up the gear and hope we can take our separate ways without getting eaten."

Delver and Roe both winced; Kestrel just raised skeptical eyebrows at him.

"Well. Not literally."

"How are you going to handle your half of things?" Delver asked. "That's an impossible climb, and not a foothold in sight."

A wry laugh escaped Kestrel before she could think, and she gestured to Shale. "He talks to rocks. I can fly. We'll manage."

Chapter Twenty-Five

Trailing a thin cable behind her, Kestrel flew to the top of the cliff and began looking for an anchor point. Below her, Shale was examining the rock, which seemed to consist of running his palms over the surface and frowning a lot. After the battle at the camp, she trusted his skills enough to leave him to it.Shale thought he could coax steps out of the rock, and her job was to get a safety line in place.

Kestrel backwinged to a stop and dropped to a landing. The grass around her was thick and vivid green, almost unnaturally so for this time of year. Rib-high plants with broad, flat leaves rose in front of her, but their crisp stems were too fragile to take Fisher's weight, let alone hers or Shale's. Once she found a reliable anchor, she'd use the line to pull up the sturdy rope that had been too heavy for her hawk-self to lift.

As she left the cliff's edge behind, the velvety-short grass at her feet rose to bushes and a few delicate trees with shimmering pastel bark. Beyond them was another smooth, sand-colored wall, this one low and irregular, rising no higher than a greenblood house's rooftop. She took a cautious sniff, then another, detecting nothing that smelled dangerous. Pleasant, in fact, a heady herbal scent that made her want to sit and breathe it in.

Reason enough for caution right there, even if most carnivorous plants used sweet or meaty smells for their lures.

She crouched into lynx form—compact, quick, and camouflaged—and prowled into the underbrush in search of a tree or rock to anchor her rope. The grass whispered under her paws, and she cast a dubious glance at it; it was all a single species as far as she could see, something that didn't happen without human interference or the kind of corruption that made a single species grow out of control. Above her head, broad leaves shifted on shining, succulent stems; she wove through them to a sunny patch of open grass beyond.

Mostly grass; level with the ground was a smooth stone basin scored by jagged cracks and surrounded by short, slender pillars. A path led further on, a winding, cobbled thing of a frivolity at odds with the stark plains below. The pillars had the same glassy smoothness as the cliff face, but they were small enough that she might be able to use them for her rope; returning to her human form, she set her shoulder against one and shoved.

And sprang back in lynx-shape as it chimed at her in rising tones, muted colors chasing themselves up the shaft where she'd touched it. Kestrel backed away, hissing.

The chimes faded and the colors dulled. A touch of one front paw to the pillar made no change, but a shift of her shape and a careful forefinger brought her a soft trill and a fleeting shimmer of blue-green-gold. Intended for humans, then, whatever it was. But the *important* thing was that it was stable enough for her anchor line.

She looped her rope around the base of the tallest pillar, turned, and went back toward the cliff's edge, waves of fragrance rippling around her as she shouldered her way through the broadleaved plants. At her wave from above, Athren tied the second line to the thin cable she'd drawn up, and she repeated the process. The pillar hummed when she accidentally bumped it with a knuckle, and she scowled at it. "Stop that. It's creepy."

She took to the air and glided down to meet the others, coasting past Shale's half-created pathway. Athren was sorting through his saddlebags, Otter was sprawled comfortably in the sun, and Shale was sitting crosslegged on a dusty patch of earth, one hand spread on the ground in what she'd come to recognize as a calming gesture. She dropped down to sit beside him. "What's the matter?"

"Hard to explain." He frowned. "Usually it takes me hours to...reach stone that I'm not familiar with. But here it's, it's awake, it's glad to see me. Blight, Kess, it feels like an old dog who sees you coming home."

"And this is bad?"

"No. But it doesn't make sense. Pebbles are one thing, but something this big should take a while to...to talk to me, not be jumping in my lap like a puppy." He shook his head. "But it doesn't feel malicious, and it's certainly easy to work with. Just be ready to jump if it wags its tail too hard."

She eyed the narrow ridge that stitched halfway up the cliff face. "How precisely do you mean that 'jump'?"

"Blight if I know."

Shale clambered to his feet and dusted himself off, offering a companionable hand to Kestrel to pull her back up. She watched curiously as he laid both palms against the cliff face, the smooth surface wrinkling under the slow pressure of magic she could barely feel. The path turned back on itself as it climbed in a series of switchbacks, each leg just wide enough for a single climber. Kestrel was fairly sure she'd rather fly up on her own than face all that yawning space with only two feet to balance on, but with the safety line in place it would be enough for a cautious climber.

Athren took leather straps from his saddlebags and began buckling them into an arcane array that eventually resolved itself into a simple harness. "Shale will use this on the way up," he said, knotting and reknotting the rope to a metal ring at the waist, "and then lower it back for the next person. I don't guess you'll need it, but I'll have to stay below to fix it for Fisher and Otter."

"We can handle it better on four feet," Otter said. His shoulders twitched toward a defensive curl. "I don't change often, but that doesn't mean I *can't*."

Athren nodded absently, snapping the harness between his hands to test its strength. "That'd make the climb easier. Probably safer, too."

So Kestrel flapped wearily to the cop of the cliff, keeping a close watch on the safety line as Shale climbed the switchbacks with one hand on the stone for balance. It might have been the glare of the afternoon sun, but halfway up she began wondering if the stone was lifting him as he climbed. Fisher scampered cheerfully up behind him, while Otter made his way more slowly in his namesake form. The river otter couldn't move as nimbly as Fisher, but the thick, sturdy claws gave him safe purchase all the way up. Still, Kestrel didn't relax until all four of them were atop the cliff with her and Athren had shrugged out of the harness.

"I think I could've skipped all that," he said to Shale. "If you slipped, the rock around here would likely reach out and catch you."

"It might." Shale didn't look particularly pleased with the notion.

"Is that a bad thing?" Kestrel asked again.

"Maybe. What if I hurt its feelings?"

"I see your point." She began to coil the rope back up, tucking her hair behind her ears as the dry wind from below blew it across her eyes. "This isn't like any place I've ever seen. No animals I've seen or scented, nothing dangerous that I can find, just-" She shook her head. "It's too blighted nice."

Athren blinked. "Oh. It's *nice*. Whatever will we do?"

"When was the last time you saw something harmless that humans or 'blood hadn't fought to get that way? There's no human scent up here, but it looks like somebody planned this place. We've got to go carefully."

Kestrel gestured them toward the broadleaved plants, which were coated with soft, fine hairs now that she saw them from above. They released another wave of fragrance as she passed them; as Shale stepped through the leaves a pace behind her, it changed to something lighter and sweeter. "Huh. Flowers."

She turned, testing the air. "It changed?"

"Guess so. It just started up when I stepped in." He took a luxurious sniff. "I like it."

It didn't seem dangerous. But Kestrel hung back while Athren pushed through the plants and their aroma changed to something warm and leathery, and kept a close eye on Fisher's black head bobbing through just under the leaves ("Candy!"). Otter's passage triggered a cool and faintly salty scent that neither of them could describe, and Kestrel ran an experimental finger over the leaves when he passed. The scent changed again to the first one she'd encountered, and Kestrel shook her head. "I like this one the best. But how does it know?"

Otter shrugged. "Ask a greenblood."

"I don't think the greenbloods have seen anything like this." Shale paused, staring down at the cracked stone basin. "I know I haven't."

"If there were humans up here, I'd think it was a fountain," Kestrel said. "People would need water from somewhere up here."

"I don't think there have been people here for a long time." Shale's face was growing slack, his eyes taking on the distant look of a beastblood deep in communion with their charges. "Hundreds of years, maybe more. They built here, and the stone misses them."

"Built what? Where?" Nothing but smooth grass under them and smooth stone before them; she could see no traces of habitation, not even ruins.

"All of this." Before she or Athren could stop him, Shale crouched to brush his fingertips over the edge of the basin; it thrummed when he touched it, waves of rosy color spreading out from the contact. "They weren't really proud of it," he said distantly. "Nothing like the *real* displays back home, just a place to rest after heavy spellwork. They woke the stone, and it doesn't know why they didn't come back. It's lonely."

Athren shook him a heartbeat before Kestrel reached him. "I don't care who it misses, the stone doesn't get *you*."

Shale rubbed a hand over his eyes until they focused again. "I know. I'm not—it's just so old, and the memories are so clear."

"What memories?" Kestrel asked.

He frowned, searching for words. "Broken things, now. Forgotten toys. Butterflies the size of your head, that died on the stone when there was nothing left to sustain them. Glowing flowers. Singing fish that lasted until the stone cracked and their pond dried, after. Cats with fur that tinkled when you stroked it. Some things are still here."

Kestrel drew in a sharp breath against the chill in her belly. "If those are toys, what did they have for defenses?"

"Nothing," Shale said simply, most of his attention still on memories from centuries ago. "They were too powerful to need them, until they weren't. And then they sealed themselves inside the rock."

"Well," Athren said after a moment, fingers drumming against his leg. "I guess we know where we're going next."

Chapter Twenty-Six

The cobbled path led them gradually away from the cliff's edge, winding through cascading vines with hard-edged leaves that tinkled as they brushed each other and trees with broad, flat branches shaped for sitting. Kestrel and Fisher prowled around the other three in fox-shape, straining ears and noses for any hint of danger. Something vast slept far below them, a dull rumble of predatory intent with no target, but beyond that she could catch only faint, unfamiliar scraps of animal thought. Once she caught a glimpse of something like an attenuated housecat, with misty-looking fur that shimmered from green to brown and back as it crept out of the leaves and down the tree trunk, but for the most part they were alone. This place had been beautiful once, but it had never been whole; to Kestrel's animal-attuned senses it felt sad and stunted, and the droop of Fisher's ears suggested that she felt the same.

Kestrel trotted ahead when the trees began to thin, the shifting breeze bringing her hints of soil and metal under the sweetly dusty smell of leaf litter and the distant tang of water. Something fluttered down to investigate her—a tiny horse the length of her fox-body, with broad black wings, forefeet that spread into avian talons, and hawk-gold eyes in a dainty equine face. She reached out with a cautious mental touch; it snorted and darted back up in a startled rattle of feathers.

"Took you long enough to find a horse that likes you," Otter snickered from behind her. She growled at him and pushed forward through the undergrowth. The leaves crunched under her feet with a muted, crystalline crackle as she padded out to open ground.

No welcoming garden here; this was the entrance to a fortress. There were obvious arrow-slits in the wall before them, offset by short, slim towers perfectly placed for archers. The vines she'd come through laced themselves through spined stone walls, their leaves turning razor edges toward anyone who approached. There was no door whatsoever, just a crude outline engraved on the face of the wall before them, burned and scarred by a long-ago assault. Kestrel tilted her head, considering, and turned to Shale as he stomped his way out of the vines. "I think this is your problem."

"I think you're right." Unconcerned, Shale held out a hand with a murmured "would you mind?"

The stone rippled as he spoke, folding back on itself to reveal a smooth-edged arch that led directly into the cliffside. Columns of smooth white rock ran from floor to ceiling; they lit up when Shale took a step forward, others flickering alight behind them to reveal a wide, spiraling ramp down.

Otter scooped Fisher up in one arm. "Oh, this doesn't look like trouble in the *least*. Kess, anything down there you can feel?"

"No. Maybe."

Athren crossed his arms and waited.

"It comes and goes. Feels like a predator, but it's not an animal and I can't hear it think."

"Can you control it?"

"Maybe. But I can't find out without letting it know I'm here."

"And you're sure it's going to start hunting 'bloods?"

"Whatever it is, it needs to feed on something to keep going, and that makes it close enough to a predator for me to feel it. If it's hungry now, that's not going to just go away."

"For what it's worth," Shale said, "the stone's on our side. It's been lonely."

Otter's mouth quirked skeptically, but he hoisted Fisher to a more secure perch and stepped forward to stand with Kestrel. "Kess in the front and I'll take rear?"

Fisher yapped at him.

"You need to stay in the middle and keep an eye on Athren," he told her solemnly.

She flattened her ears suspiciously but scrambled down and trotted into position behind Kestrel.

The walls inside were marked at intervals by singed, scarred patches, flaking away here and there to reveal sharp-edged gashes. Rough patches of stone were vertically arranged in a way that made her think of the arrow-slits outside, and she eyed them warily as she passed. Beyond that, they showed no trace of human handiwork, stretching away glass-smooth and seamless as far as she could see. Dust piled in velvety drifts along the floor, and one glance down convinced her that it was useless to try hiding their passage. Deep as it was, there was no way to hide their prints; any attempt might hide their numbers but not their presence. And something down there...echoed. Not quite thought, not quite emotion, just a mental pressure like a memory given will.

"Shale? What do you think?"

Fingertips skimming the wall, he gave her a distracted glance. "No threat that I can feel, and the stone doesn't remember anything happening for—I don't know how long. Longer than any of us have been alive. Whoever lived here, they were lower down."

Kestrel wasn't reassured. *Something* was below them or ahead of them; nothing she could identify, but it resonated enough with the hunters she knew that she could sense its presence. Something that had to take life to survive, and the only reason it wasn't hunting them was that it hadn't caught their scent. So she kept a wary silence as they crept further into the ruin. Just at the edge of hearing, she could catch a thumping sound like a slow heartbeat, deep and persistent, and she kept one ear trained on it as they descended.

The ramp branched out into a collection of halls with horizontal slits near the ceiling and a complex array of chambers on each side. The layout looked to her like greenblood dormitories, but any furnishings had long since rotted into dust. Plaques set at head-height at every door reminded her of the healer's hall in Threeshores, but where the healers had set mosaics in the wall to show the room's contents, these had...markings. Delicate little traceries like bird tracks in the snow, almost decorative but too irregular for her to consider beautiful. She frowned at them.

"Athren? Any idea what this is about?"

He ran his fingers over a plaque and its collection of incised curves and angles. "Not sure. Sometimes master glassworkers would stamp their work with something like this—not as complicated, though. I have no idea how you'd remember to draw one of these, much less make a stamp of it."

"Not stamps," Shale said, his eyes narrow as he tried to sort through centuries-old thoughts. "Someone made each mark, and the marks...talked, more or less. There were more in the middle of this level, and people went there to learn things. I don't know how."

Led by Shale's hazy direction, they found an expansive room, thickly set with glowing columns of rock and stone shelves carved out of every wall. The distant pulse Kestrel had been hearing thumped in her ears even in human form; it was unpleasant, but at least she could use it to orient herself. Dust coated the shelves even more deeply than the floors, and when Kestrel swept a hand along them, she raised nothing more than a nose-stinging cloud.

Shale frowned. "They stored up knowledge here, I can *see* it. People sitting with things that look like stacks of cloth, and the cloth told them things somehow. Like the Riders' map back in Threeshores; it's not the real thing but it tells you about it."

"Shale." Athren laid a hand on his brother's arm, conflict clear in the pace of his breathing and the set of his shoulders. "I want to know all this too, but if Kess is right, there's something down here that wants to *eat* us all. We can't stay to puzzle it out."

"But no one's ever been here. No one may ever make it back again."

"I want to learn too. I *also* want to not get eaten. We deal with whatever's down there and we can come back-" He glanced at Kestrel. She nodded. "And take some time to study. But it's too dangerous to go without you, and we can't leave you in a trance, looking for knowledge that's a thousand years dead!"

Slowly, Shale closed his eyes, letting his breath out in a rigidly controlled exhalation. "You're right. Blight it. But stone this old, with nothing to cover up the memories—I'm not leaving this place until I've had some time to talk with it."

Kestrel held out a hand for him as he rose. "Are you all right?"

"Mostly. Hard to tell where to go, with all the years between us and whoever was here last. Like trying to fish in molasses."

The maze of narrow halls and chambers was too complex to explore, so they relied on Shale's instincts to take them further down. His steps slowed and he stumbled more than once, more and more of his attention focused on his connection to the stone; after the second stumble, Kestrel took to cat-form so he could steady himself with one hand on her back. Between her ears and the buried memories Shale relayed, they picked their way through the tangled corridors and to another carved door-outline like the one they'd entered through. It parted soundlessly for Shale when he was still a manheight away.

Kestrel and Fisher both hunched and flattened their ears at the sudden thunderous din from below; the others, with less sensitive ears, only winced. After a heart-pounding moment, she recognized the same persistent rhythm that had been vibrating through her paws—closer now and louder, with a steady beat too unchanging to belong to anything living. She'd thought it might belong to the sleeping hunter below, but her tentative mental exploration showed her no connection.

"Sounds like a glasswright's bellows," Athren said. "Just a couple dozen times bigger."

"I've *seen* those bellows," Shale grumbled. "That's not reassuring."

"What would a bellows that size even be for?" Otter asked.

"Ventilation, maybe." Athren gestured at the slits near the ceiling. "Otherwise we might not be able to breathe down here at all."

There was no imposing ramp down here, just a utilitarian staircase with a gradual curve, sparsely lit by glowing columns as they followed it down and further down. Deeper than Threeshores was tall, the stairs turning around a central shaft with that great booming pulse somewhere within...Kestrel's ears pulled tight against her head as she tried not to think of breaking walls and splintering machinery. Below her, something shifted, vague memories of battle and defense blundering through her mind like moths throwing themselves at a windowpane.

"I think it's a pump," Athren said after a few flights. She glanced backward and saw him carrying a weary Fisher in the crook of one arm. "We saw a stream when we came in, and a clever enough artisan could redirect water to drive—well, something—and let it flow on from there. I just don't know how it's lasted this long."

"Metal and magic." Shale's voice sounded scratchy and distant. "It's powered by moving water like any miller's wheel, but crafting that pump was beyond anything stoneblood can do. Even all of us put together."

She could smell the water from somewhere below, laced with salt and strange accents as subtle and layered as a tapestry. To a feline nose it was dizzyingly complex; even in human form Otter was taking deep, curious breaths.

Athren made a thoughtful noise. "They weren't regular people, then?"

"Human, maybe. They weren't 'blood. And I don't know where they got their power."

The stairs ended with a blunt efficiency that owed little to design and everything to practicality. At the bottom was a trio of small stone rooms set in the central shaft, their doors and furnishings long since rotted away. The last room, empty as the others, was lined with stone shelves and had a narrow passageway in the back wall. Kestrel turned toward it instinctively, drawn by the sharpening scent of water.

"Probably access for whoever tended the machinery," Athren said, coming up behind her to investigate. She gave him a raspy not-quite-growl and butted her head against his hip. "All right, I know, you go first. You've got the teeth in case something goes wrong."

She lifted her chin and tail in a housecat's smug gesture and padded ahead, sorting through the unfamiliar mix of scents as she walked. Metal, stone, that salty-cool water smell, utterly different from streams or swamps, and—warm bark? Leaves? Something green that shouldn't be this far underground.

She rumbled a warning to Athren and slunk forward, ears flat and shoulders hunched to create a low profile. The passage opened up into the shaft itself, crystals pouring sun-bright light onto an enormous metal pump and the two figures beneath it.

Hackles raised, Kestrel hissed and sprang backward, and behind her Athren made a choking noise. For the first time in her life, she grasped the fear that humans felt of her own kind.

Chapter Twenty-Seven

The first figure, a jagged assortment of sticks in a roughly human shape, didn't move. But the second turned jerkily toward them. She smelled human but *wrong*, all normal scents overpowered by a stinging, dusty aroma of overgrown bark. Her joints were knobbly and coated in seamed, rough bark that extended out from wrists, elbows and knuckles, terminating in clumsy, wood-hard fingertips. Her face was covered in smooth growth like a sapling's bark beneath a viny tangle that might be hair; tiny ferns like lashes surrounded her wide brown eyes. Ears flat and tail lashing, Kestrel shouldered Athren back and angled herself across the corridor.

"Kess!" Otter called from somewhere behind her.

She snarled a warning, the sound lost in the drumming thunder of the pipe, and took another step backward.

"Don't go!" The woman levered herself painfully to her feet. To her feet, and no further; shackles twined with thorny vines ran from her wrists to the puddle of briny water on the floor. She brushed distractedly at them. "You're 'blood, aren't you? Real ones?"

"She's real," Athren answered; no point in denying *that* whether Kestrel was in cat-shape or out of it. "I'm just a friend. Who are you?"

"I'm—I was-" She drew a breath, and Kestrel tried to ignore the subtle creaking sounds just at the edge of hearing. "My name is Fern."

Athren looked down at her. "This what you've been tracking, Kess?"

She tucked her chin in a curt negative, and came reluctantly out of cat-form a second later. "I didn't know she was here until I smelled her just now. Whatever the danger is, it's still here and it hasn't noticed us yet."

"He will," the woman said, and then corrected herself with a dazed shake of her head. "It. They will. Sometimes both, I can't—it's hard to tell. But it comes every day at sunrise."

"How do you know?" Athren asked, looking at the towering, windowless shaft above them.

"I'm greenblood," she said simply. "I know."

In the antechamber to the pump shaft, the greenblood woman paced carefully, eyes wide with wonder and a little fear as she reaccustomed herself to movement. The wood and metal chains still trailed from her wrists, but at Shale's request the stone beneath her had loosened its hold on their anchors. He was prowling the edges of the room now, fingers spread as if connected to the earth by invisible lines. One sudden move, and Kestrel had no doubt the greenblood would find herself caged again.

"I never believed in ghosts," Fern said. "But may the Death burn me if I can find any other way to say it. I call it the Eldest just to have a word for it, but I'm not sure how many it—they—are. It thinks it's male most of the time, but sometimes it looks and sounds female." She breathed out hard, and Kestrel thought she would have shuddered if she still could. "It gets in your mind, it can make you want what it wants however hard you fight, but it can't keep control every moment." She lifted one shackled wrist by way of explanation.

"So what does it want?"

"A body." Kestrel snarled, and Fern flinched. "Not mine. Or yours. It's been making me—grow one, I suppose you'd say—since I first came here. It's been getting faster the last few—years, maybe? It found a Rider that hunts 'blood for it to drain, so it can build power to animate the body."

"How long have you been here?" Otter asked. "And how'd you find it?"

"You saw the plants up above? I felt them on the plains and wanted to investigate. I called the vines down to lift me up; when they did, it just seemed like I should walk to the fortress wall, and so I did. After that-" She broke off with a pained shrug. "By the time I controlled my own body again, I was down here. There's algae and tiny plants in the water that runs through this pump; I've been pouring every bit of power I could into them and sending them out to grow, hoping that someone would notice and come to investigate."

"For how long?"

"A few tree generations; I can't tell beyond that. What year is it?"

Kestrel and Otter traded glances of mutual incomprehension.

"I was born two hundred and ten years after the Death. How many has it been now?"

"We don't know what you're talking about," Athren said carefully.

She paled, and the viny mass of her hair pulled in on itself. "They tell us stories about it when we're young. The earth split, the plants died and came back thorned or venomous or *hungry,* and the beasts don't bear thinking about. It was years before the survivors could even think about marking time, and you don't *know*?"

Otter shook his head. "Nothing in beastblood stories."

"Rumors," Shale said after a moment's thought. "Just a grain of a story here or there. The oldest stones I've ever touched remembered fear and magic, but nothing else."

"Nobody was able to keep records on paper, but they carved it into wood and wove it into tapestries to keep at Farwatch. There should be *something.*"

"Oh." Shale bit his lip. "Farwatch...died. A long time ago."

Kestrel slipped out of cat-form with an irritated flick of her tail. "Not the point. We know we've got an enemy, we know what it wants, and we *don't* know how to stop it."

"There's still time," Fern said. "The body it wants is mostly alive, but there isn't enough power yet to make it move. There's a passage down from here that leads to level ground; I can feel it every time the pump draws water in. There's still time to run-"

Kestrel showed her teeth. "I'm not running."

"You *can*," Fern said with a bitter glance at her shackled wrists. "I've wanted to every time I've been conscious enough to think, but there's never been a chance. And when I wake up, it's not long before the Eldest comes."

"If it drains power, then yours may be what keeps it awake enough to act instead of...lurking," Shale said.

Athren looked around the crowded chamber, eyes narrowed. "So we try and clear an escape route in case we need it. I'll stay here with Fern and Fisher, and you three make sure there's an open exit. Preferably one with nothing appalling between us and it. *Then* we try to put together a battle plan."

Once past the pump column, the passage they'd been following broadened and began to angle slightly downward. The dust had thinned into near-nonexistence somewhere on the stairs, but down here the moisture in the air fed algae that coated the walls in a thin sheen. Kestrel didn't consider it an improvement; the rank green smell didn't quite drown out the scent of water ahead of them, but it made it hard to sniff out any living dangers. Shale was untroubled, but Otter was hesitating for a deep breath with every few steps, eyes wide with curiosity and...excitement?

"Are you alright?" She bumped companionably against his shoulder.

"For now." He scowled into the darkness ahead of them, then shook his head and looked back at her. "There's something nearby—somethings—I can't hear them thinking, but I can feel them a little. Kess, there's so *many*."

"Part of our ghost?" She couldn't feel that hungry presence any more clearly down here, but she didn't want to be surprised.

"I don't think so. They're not paying attention to anything in here, much less us."

Troubled, she quickened her step to catch up with Shale. "Otter says there's some sort of creatures close to us, maybe outside and maybe not. He doesn't know what they are, but keep an ear out."

He nodded. "Likely it's the animals in whatever river that pump draws from. There's nothing living in here but us."

"Good," she said fervently. "I'm getting tired of secrets and surprises."

"It remembers, though," Shale said absently. "The stone keeps trying to convince me that I'm a trainee that's forgotten where he's supposed to be."

"A trainee what?"

"Soldier?" His voice wrapped uncertainly around the unfamiliar word. "Like a guardsman in some sort of oversized warband. They were—other soldiers were hunting them, and they hid here..." He trailed off. "That's all I can tell without sitting down and really listening, and we don't have time for that."

"We don't. Sorry."

He tipped his head in acknowledgment and continued down the passageway. Even without seeing his eyes, she could tell from his pace and the set of his shoulders that most of his attention was on images hundreds of years old. "They brought their supplies in on boats and pulled them up through this passage." His hands shaped the words until she could almost see crates and carts dragging their way up the sloping passage. "Food, weapons, sacrifices, fuel...new recruits brought it all in and put it up, until there were no more new recruits and no more shipments. Eventually, no more people; the last of them deserted and left only their commanders. And the commanders went up top and-" He flinched with a sudden sharp sound of distress. "The walls can't tell me what happened after that. It hurts."

He swayed a bit on his next step, and she tucked her arm around his elbow. "Can you just—not listen?"

"To the stone? It just likes having me here, it's not trying to tell me stories. That was all my own blighted curiosity."

"Well, try to be bored for a little bit. We can't afford to risk any of us now."

He made a noncommittal noise but straightened his shoulders and jammed his hands into his pockets. Kestrel glanced over her shoulder to Otter, who stepped up to pace the stoneblood on his other side.

"I know what you're doing, you know," Shale grumbled.

"We know," Otter said cheerfully. "Survive first, study later, all right?"

The passage ended abruptly in front of another outlined door. Shale touched cautious fingertips to it, frowned for a long moment, and gestured to Kestrel. "Here. I need your hand."

She raised her eyebrows but let him guide her to lay her palm against the shallow carving. He covered her hand with his own, and for a moment the smooth rock prickled under her skin before he released her and did the same with Otter.

"There. For the next few days it'll open for either of you the same way it would for me. If something happens, you'll still be able to run."

Brows furrowed, Otter spread his fingers against the door, and it eased away from his touch. A cool, steady wind pushed in from outside, bringing with it a repetitive rushing sound and a breeze loaded with strange smells. She could see a flat, pebbly surface just outside the arch, gleaming damply in the starlight.

Otter drew a sudden, startled breath. "That's *it*, Kess, that's what I've been feeling." His eyes were impossibly bright, his fingers flexing as if trying to reshape themselves into paws or flippers.

She sniffed: salt, brackish water, and complex layers of growth and decay. Something smelled vaguely animal, but not the musky, leafy scents she was accustomed to. She was curious, but nowhere near curious enough to explore while she still had family inside.

"I have to see what it is, Kess. I have to know."

"Not *yet!* If we trust Fern, we've got till sunrise to fight this thing or run. If we don't trust her, we've got less."

Half-turned to rush forward, he froze in place. After an anxious moment, he breathed out hard and closed his eyes. "I know. It's important. There's things calling me out there that I never knew existed...but it's you and Fisher in here, and I know what I have to do. But if we make it through, I'm not leaving until I know what's past that door."

Chapter Twenty-Eight

"If it finds me gone by sunrise, it'll start looking for me and probably find all of you," Fern said. "Hundreds of years I've been trapped here, and now it comes down to one night."

"How did you survive?" Athren asked.

"Mostly I drew on the plants up top. I guess that's why..." She held her twiggy fingers up in explanation. "A few years ago it pulled in some wandering Rider, and he brought me rations when he wasn't out hunting for the Eldest. I really don't remember much—working when it had control of me, half-asleep most of the time."

"Does it ever talk to you? Anything we can use?" Shale asked. "What does it want?"

Fern frowned, face lifting to focus on something none of them could see. "It wants—they want—to *hurt*. All of them are angry, one or two are guilty, but even those want to get back at the people who drove them to...whatever they did."

"Who are long gone," Otter pointed out.

"I don't think it matters."

"We can't let it loose," Shale said flatly. "If it has even a fraction of the power that built this place, it'd be worse than plague and wildfire together. The stone remembers deserters, and what happened to the ones who got caught. I'm not talking about it with Fisher here, but after what I saw I'd believe any evil of these people."

"It's not 'people'," Kestrel said. "If it were human, I couldn't feel it like I do." And wished she didn't; that constant sensation of a predator shifting in its sleep was frightening and exhausting. "It's intelligent in its way, but it doesn't *think*, it's just hungry."

"Reassuring," Shale muttered, and she shared a wry half-smile with him.

Fern's fingers ticked softly as she interlaced them. "The trouble is, I know about you now and I won't be able to hide that when it comes again."

"I may be able to alter its perceptions," Kestrel volunteered. "A little. Maybe enough to hide us, maybe not. My mother was able to stay out of its notice by thinking more like an animal than a human—I might be able to do something similar."

"I've been here too long; it'll know if I'm not where it left me. And it's got a connection to the body I built, it just hasn't got the power to bring it to life. If it can draw on all of you..." She hesitated, head down. "It might *win*. After all this time, I don't want it to get away with what it did to me."

Kestrel nodded in heartfelt understanding. "So how do we kill it?"

"That's where I fail. All that time with that thing in my mind, in my *magic*, and I was never able to find a weakness."

Otter reached out a hand in tentative comfort. "You did say it kept you dazed. If we let it have the body, could we kill that?"

Fern's eyes widened. "No. We don't dare let it take an actual form. Some of the hints it's dropped over the years...I *know* they raised this cliff out of flat ground over just a few days. The weapons it's talked about drew on more magic than a clan of greenbloods could muster." She shook her head. "Give it form for even a moment, and it might turn us all to ash."

Fisher flinched back into Otter's lap; he smoothed her hair back absently. "So we can't kill it. Can we contain it?"

"How? Short of bringing the cliff down-"

"*Weeks*," Shale said, glancing up at the mass of stone above their heads.

Containment, Kestrel thought, and swallowed down a sudden surge of fear. "Shale, can I have a word with you? Alone?"

They retreated into the pump shaft, where the rumble of machinery drowned out their voices. "That map-stone you made for Athren," Kestrel said. "Is it attuned to you? Like the teaching stones you talked about before?"

"More. I built it up from sand to get the details just ri-" He gave her a narrow-eyed look. "Why do you want to know?"

"Because." She gathered herself. "I think we can get Fern out of here and trap it while it's looking for her. But it has to be you and me, and the rest aren't going to like it."

"Why?"

She told him.

He took an uneasy half-step back. "You're right, they won't like it. *I* don't like it."

"But will you back me up?"

"Yes."

Otter swore. And shouted until Fisher hid behind Athren's legs. And asked whether Kestrel was planning to leave *him* to explain to their mother if things went wrong. Even Athren looked doubtful, but said only, "It's decent tactics" when she pressed him.

"Look, I'm not *trying* to get killed," she told Otter in exasperation. "We've got one chance to take this thing by surprise, and I can't think of any other way to do it."

"If there were time-"

"There's not."

"*Blight*." His sigh sounded more like a snarl than anything else, but he pulled Kestrel close in a quick, hard embrace. "That's not because I like what you're doing, it's so I don't hate myself later for not doing it."

"I'll try to stick around so you're good and embarrassed."

"You do that."

He lifted Fisher up for her own hug and then turned to Shale. "Get her out safe. Drag her by the scruff if she won't listen."

"Do my best. Get Fern well clear, and if you don't see us by noon tomorrow, run for Threeshores any way you can. Haila's got 'blood friends everywhere and she knows Athren; she'll believe what we found and mount whatever defense she can."

"Just be careful."

Athren snorted. "Don't be careful, be *right*."

Spine rigid, Otter nodded to Shale, thumped Kestrel awkwardly on the shoulder, and took Fisher's hand on his way out to the passage. Athren hesitated, then simply handed his miniature map to Shale. "Hope it works. I'd rather have you than a map."

"Yeah. So would I."

As his brother left, Shale threaded a cord through the hole in the top of the map and handed it to Kestrel. "That going to fit?"

"It needs to be shorter," she said, slipping it around her neck and knotting it more closely. "Wolf-size, not human."

"Wolf? I figured you'd be going with a hawk. Familiarity, and all that."

"I thought about it. But the wolf gives me the best chance—nothing else has the kind of bonds I'll need."

"All right." He squeezed her hands once. "Luck to you, Kess."

"To both of us. If I don't make it out, tell Otter not to be mad. And to find a good teacher for Fisher. And-"

"I'll tell him."

She nodded and turned away. "All right. Keep an ear out but don't come where I can see you if you can help it. The less I notice, the better our chances are."

She heard him step toward the door as she gathered herself. He didn't say another word, and she was grateful; words were quite precisely the last thing she needed now. Shoulders squared, she walked into the room where Fern had been imprisoned for decades, letting wolf-form and wolf-thought wash over her until there was nothing left but purpose and the pack.

Chapter Twenty-Nine

Head low and ears swiveling, the wolf paced the confines of the small pump room, wrinkling her muzzle at the brackish smell of the pool in its center. A wolf alone was ineffective, but something down here threatened her pack, and she was the hunter best suited to deal with it. The new female had the knowledge but wasn't fierce enough to fight, and neither her brothers nor the cub had sharp enough teeth or a quick enough leap for this enemy. She had to be ready for the ambush, then find her pack again if she could.

Under the constant burr and clang of the vast metal cylinder, she could hear a faint, comforting gurgle of moving water, but there was no sound to indicate either predator or prey nearby. Beside the pool stood a pile of sticks that almost looked human; it made her want to snarl, though she didn't know why. Dead wood couldn't endanger her or her pack.

But there was something down here that could, and soon it would be close enough for her to spring on it. Her brother, cub-sister, and all but one of the rest were safe on the open trail; the other male was nearby but might be able to run if she failed. She had the strongest jaws in her little pack, and she wouldn't let her enemy pass. Till then, there was only patience.

Ears and eyes on the single entrance, she arranged herself belly-down on the cool stone and waited.

Time passed. Time was nothing to a wolf. She changed position once, twice, to keep her muscles limber and her senses sharp, but she kept her golden stare fixed on the door until some distant disturbance alerted senses no normal wolf should have. A faint shimmer of movement disturbed the air in front of her.

There was nothing to smell. There was hardly anything to see, only a vague human outline made of dust motes and droplets of moisture. But there was enough for the wolf to see surprise and dismay as the figure reached out searchingly, recoiled, and cast around for the source of power it had expected. The wolf's hackles lifted and she backed away, but not soon enough to keep her eyes from meeting the other's attention. It struck out at her with crashing force like whitewater over a river rock, and she yelped in surprise. Power like hooks scraped over her mind, power like the reek of slumbervine billowed around her...power intended to overwhelm a human receded from the wolf's mind without effect, and she snarled. She knew this prey. She could bring it down.

Her claws scraped against the floor as she lunged with body and mind at once, locking her jaws around the woody throat as she pulled a ghostly, fragmented consciousness to her own. Cub-killer, wildfire, foaming sickness: the words were beyond the wolf's mind, but she flung the images at the intruder as quickly and furiously as snapping teeth. Bark shattered under her jaws and splinters of alien memory battered at her mind.

Growing desperation, starvation while siege weapons shake the walls and the earth, rage that conceals fear that conceals hatred.

"We're losing. We've lost. Got to take the books and run. They'll sacrifice any of us they catch-"

"No. I'll bring this place down on our heads and theirs first."

Her claws left furrows in the mossy stone as the mental battering transformed to raw physical power that swatted her away. She spun against the wall and lunged again.

Deserters creeping away in the dead of night and then in daylight, caught between fear of the enemy and fear of their commanders.

"Scorched earth, haven't you incompetents ever heard of that? If we can't keep the territory, we'll leave it useless."

"That's not useless, it's poisoned!"

"Even better."

Images of a ritual, elaborate words and gestures she didn't understand, shot through with bitterness, spite, fear.

Illusory images boiled wildly out from the presence in the room as it cast about for anything to distract her: fire, lightning, ranks of men bearing weapons that neither the wolf nor the human at her core comprehended. Ears flat, she lowered her head and charged through them until her teeth met around a core of living wood.

"They'll kill any magic-user they see after this, right down to the hedge-witches and astrologers."

"What difference will that make to us?"

And an outpouring of venomous skill and power that frayed the fabric of the world, twisting everything that lived for centuries in a single moment of malice. The wolf's mind flickered with a rising snarl of equal parts disbelief and anger.

Kinless freaks, you broke the world for spite?

Her mind somewhere between wolf and woman, she pursued the hostile, fragmented mind down through indecipherable flashes of memory and pounced. Wood splintered under her teeth as the other consciousness wriggled in her mental jaws, flooding her with waves of rage and resentment and clawing for control of her mind. Her forelegs splayed at the edge of the pool as she panted for breath. *My mind. My pack. My world.*

"Kestrel. *Kess!*"

Dazed, she looked up to see a human male across the room. The scent was familiar, the voice said *pack*.

Shale?

She glanced down in confusion at the stone disc that thrummed over her ruff.

Shale skidded around the pool and dropped to his knees beside her. "Ready for you. Don't botch this, or we die and he lives."

Kestrel remembered now. Friend, not pack. Beastblood, not wolf. And for all its power, the fragmented spirit she held captive was predator enough that she could control it.

She examined the tangled knot of memory and emotion: anger above all, a hint of guilt, and spiteful determination. She could calm enraged bears and heal rabid wolves; controlling a half-mad ghost wasn't such a big step up.

It struggled all the way, but she tugged its consciousness away from her own and toward Athren's stone amulet the same way she would coax an animal toward sleep. Accustomed to stoneblood magic, the map's crystalline structure absorbed what Kestrel gave it like sand taking in water, and Shale's power followed hers to seal that ancient mind behind a barrier of stone. The stone crackled and grew cold against her chest.

Shale breathed out hard. "Did we get it?"

Kestrel released the wolf-form, ignoring the tremor in her forelegs that moved to her hands, and pulled the amulet back over her head. "Maybe? Wait a second so I can check. And hit me if I don't act like me."

She cast around for any trace of that looming, hungry presence, but the hallways and stairs above felt utterly empty. "I can't feel it."

Shale tapped the amulet with a cautious finger. "Feels dead; it's like trying to connect with a fish or a leaf. I think...we may have done it."

He clambered to his feet and offered her a hand up. She accepted it after a disorienting moment of wondering why she should walk on her hind legs.

"Right," he said. "So I think we've saved the day. Now we have to go let our little brothers yell at us about it."

"Don't they get feasts and statues and things in hearthtales?"

"Think so. Me, I'll settle for some jerky and about four days to sleep."

Kestrel didn't admit to wobbling on her feet, and Shale didn't say a word about it as they left the ancient machinery behind. Drawn by the strengthening breeze from outside, they followed the passageway down to meet Otter and the rest on a flat, sandy patch of ground. On Kestrel's right, a shifting expanse of water stretched beyond the horizon, and a salt-laden breeze blew into her face. She'd never seen so much water in her life. "What is that?"

She whipped around at the clatter of feathers behind her, and caught a glimpse of white plumage and elongated wings before Otter dropped to the ground with a fledgling's graceless speed. "I don't know." He hugged her, eyes alight and an unfamiliar, irrepressible grin flickering over his face. "But it's mine."

Chapter Twenty-Nine

"You're sure it's dead? Mute? Whatever?" Otter turned the stone disc contemplatively over in his hands.

"I'm not sure it was alive to start with," Kestrel answered. "But it's contained. If Shale can't feel anything in the stone, I don't think anything's there to be felt."

They were sprawled comfortably on the sand next to that vast expanse of water, unfamiliar birds sweeping in wide white arcs above their heads. A tension she'd never noticed until it was gone had eased out of Otter's body, making him look somehow older and younger at once. His relief and Kestrel's exhaustion had left both of them disinclined to do more than just breathe the quiet morning air; Shale was in a similar state, but Fisher was scampering up and down the sand, alternating between digging up tiny mussels and bouncing along after the tiny birds that chased the waves in and out. Athren was trying to keep an ear on the conversation, aside from occasional departures to pick Fisher up when a wave knocked her off her feet.

"Good. You realize if you ever do that again, I'm going to knock you over and sit on you until you change your mind?"

Too tired to invent a suitable counter-threat, Kestrel flapped a weary hand at him and leaned back on the sand. Slowly warming under the rising sun, it felt almost as inviting as a feather bed, and she wondered idly if she could talk Athren into keeping watch for a few hours while she slept.

After they'd dealt with this last difficulty.

Fern was sitting nearby, with her arms wrapped around her knees and her face turned to the sun she hadn't seen in centuries. At Kestrel's inquiring look, she stretched her arm out to take the map on hits cord and held it for a long, thoughtful moment. "I can feel *something*, but I don't think it can feel me. Like knowing somebody's awake in the next room, but nothing more than that. The question is, what happens to it?"

"Can't destroy it," Shale said. "That'd likely give us the same problem all over again. There's a few people I'd trust to keep an eye on it, if we can get it to them."

"But how sure are we that it won't be able to influence them over time?" Athren asked. "I don't want to leave it for people to deal with a hundred years from now."

Otter cleared his throat pointedly, and gestured to the shifting expanse of water in front of them. "I can't tell you how far it goes, but I *can* tell you how deep it is. There's places down there where the light never reaches, where nothing goes but little finger-sized fish. Take it down there, and it'll be out of reach and out of any sort of influence for good."

Kestrel took a deep breath and blinked to try and drive herself back to alertness. "All right. Give me a little while to rest and I'll fly it out-"

"Kess," Otter said gently. "*Fish.* I can do this."

"But there could be something dangerous out there."

"There is. Lots. And none of it will threaten me. I can feel everything in the water, Kess. Huge fish and tiny fish and things that fly along the sand and things that look like fish but think like people. I can *do* this."

"I-"

"You don't have to protect me here. Promise." He tugged the disc out of her hands. "I'll be fine."

"You'd better be."

He kicked off his boots and waded into the salty water, knee-deep and then hip-deep. He dove forward and was gone in a metallic flash of scales, the map trailing after him on its leather cord. In the murky water, Kestrel lost sight of him in only a few heartbeats.

The sun was lowering toward evening when he came back. Kestrel wasn't *quite* pacing; it would have disturbed the others, and she was too exhausted to begin with. But when Fisher clambered into her lap, she absently ruffled the fox cub's fur until her fingers were tired, keeping a careful eye on the ever-shifting water. Still, Fisher was the first to see a human-sized, finned creature cutting through the waves, and she stood up on Kestrel's knee and yapped.

The creature was long and streamlined with smooth grey skin, horizontal tail fins, and an oversized fish in its mouth. It coasted cheerfully to shore on a cresting wave, spat out the fish, and resolved itself into a damp but thoroughly satisfied Otter. "Here. I brought dinner."

"How deep did you take it?" Kestrel asked later, sitting side by side with Otter while the fish cooked in the embers and Fisher watched it with distinctly predatory intent.

"A couple of hundred manheights, and wedged it under a rock for good measure." He smiled. "It felt good, going somewhere no one else has ever been. Ever *seen*, most likely. The dolphins say they've never seen anything like me."

She blinked. "The what?"

"Dolphins. They look like fish, but they bear live pups and nurse them, and they're smart enough to talk to. And they know so much more than I do about—all of this." He waved an enthusiastic hand at the murmuring waves in front of them, then sobered. "Kess. I can't go back yet."

She swallowed hard, feeling tears prick at her eyes for the first time since she'd come home to the smell of smoke. "Yeah. I know."

"I can't leave all this untouched, I've got to learn. I've felt so useless, and now this—you know, I didn't feel a single corrupted animal while I was out there? If I can find out what makes the water different from the land..."

"Maybe we can duplicate it."

"Or at least see what a place looks like in balance, without scrambling to correct the problems that the last fix caused." He bumped his shoulder against hers. "It shouldn't be more than a turn of the seasons, and then I can split my time between here and home. And now you know it's here, you can come over the cliffs without dealing with spooky tunnels and pushy ghosts." The understatement surprised a burst of reluctant laughter from her. "There's even raptors out here. Maybe you can learn about them and show me a few tricks."

She snorted. "Bet you I can."

"I'll have to start practicing quick, then." He leaned comfortably against her. "So I can come find you if I need you—those white birds are good distance fliers—and you can come find me. After you catch up with Mother and, um, explain the change in plans."

She squeezed her eyes shut. "Yeah, that'll be fun."

"It won't be so bad. Slow going until you can find a place to trade for a couple of mounts. But the weather should hold for a while longer, and there's no kidnapped relatives, no vengeful magical ghosts...should be an easy trip back."

Farther down the beach, Fisher plopped to an unceremonious seat in the sand, stared long and hard at the birds circling overhead, and hunched down abruptly into a puffy ball of brown juvenile feathers. She fanned her wings, hopped into the air for a few clumsy flaps, and cheeped triumphantly.

Kestrel and Otter traded looks of mutual dismay.

"Or maybe not."